More Tales from Fairyland

MORE TALES
FROM FAIRYLAND

by

Illustrated by

Gunvor Edwards

RED FOX

A Red Fox Book
Published by Random House Children's Books
20 Vauxhall Bridge Road, London SW1V 2SA

A division of Random House UK Ltd
London Melbourne Sydney Auckland
Johannesburg and agencies throughout the world

Text © Darrell Waters Ltd 1994
Illustrations © Gunvor Edwards 1994

These stories first appeared in Enid Blyton's
Sunny Stories magazine.
First published in book form by Red Fox 1994

5 7 9 10 8 6 4

Set in Plantin Roman
by Intype, London

Printed and bound in Great Britain by
Cox & Wyman Ltd, Reading, Berkshire

RANDOM HOUSE UK Limited Reg. No. 954009

ISBN 0 09 913941 3

Contents

The Cuckoo Who Stayed Behind

Once upon a time there was a naughty cuckoo called Beeko, who would *not* do as he was told. He grew up in the nest of a little hedge-sparrow, and as soon as he was big enough he began to want his own way.

'Dinner, dinner, dinner!' he screamed all day long, for he was a terribly hungry baby.

'Hush! hush!' begged his frightened foster-mother, the quiet hedge-sparrow. 'You will fetch people to the nest, and then you will perhaps be taken away and given to a cat!'

'Dinner, dinner, dinner!' screeched the disobedient young cuckoo.

The hedge-sparrow called to her husband and away they went in a hurry to find some woolly-bear caterpillars to give to the baby.

'Dinner, dinner, dinner!' called the little cuckoo, more loudly than ever. 'Quick, quick, quick!'

'Hush!' called a robin nearby. 'You'll bring all the cats and weasels of the neighbourhood here!'

'Don't care!' said the baby, rudely. 'Quick, quick, bring my dinner!'

The more he grew, the louder became his voice, and the worse his manners. The worst of it was, it was no good pecking him to punish him for his wilfulness, for he was so big that he could peck back quite easily.

In fact he soon became so big that the nest wouldn't hold him, and he had to get out and sit on the branch nearby.

He was soon much bigger than his foster-mother and father! They worked themselves to skin and bone trying to keep up with his enormous appetite.

'Really, my dear!' said the little hedge-sparrow to her husband, 'I've quite forgotten what a nice juicy worm tastes like! Beeko is so greedy that I have to give him everything!'

'He is not a nice child to have,' said the other hedge-sparrow. 'Mark my words, little wife, he will come to a bad end!'

Next day Beeko said he wanted to come out with the hedge-sparrows and see the world.

'You can't,' said the sparrows. 'You must stay at home and try and get rid of that awful voice of yours.'

'I shan't, then!' screamed Beeko in a temper. And sure enough he didn't. He flew out with them and wouldn't leave them. They were terribly upset, because he made such an awful noise that everyone looked to see what it was, and a cat woke up and came slinking near to them.

'Fly! Fly!' cried the hedge-sparrows, and the three rose in the air. Beeko couldn't fly properly, and he very nearly flew straight at the cat.

'See what a fine voice I have!' said Beeko, very much pleased.

'Fine voice indeed!' scolded the sparrows angrily. 'It was your fine voice that nearly brought us to our end. We shall be glad when you start cuckooing properly, and stop that terrible, piercing squeak!'

When Beeko was three times as big as the hedge-sparrows he flew away from them and said he didn't want to be scolded any more. He flew to a cool wood and had a perfectly

lovely time eating hundreds of caterpillars that hung from an oak tree.

'This is better than having to wait till I'm fed!' he said to himself.

Soon he met more young cuckoos and they had a fine time chasing in and out among the trees. The biggest one was the leader, and he told them all what to do.

But that didn't suit Beeko for long. *He* wasn't going to do what he was told.

'I shan't stay with you!' he said. 'I'm going off by myself!'

'But you mustn't!' cried the biggest cuckoo.

'We shall soon be going on a long journey over the sea to a lovely warm land where there are heaps of insects to eat. You must go with us!'

'Oh *must* I?' cried Beeko, ruffling up all his feathers crossly. 'Well, then I just *won't*, see! What's the matter with this land, I should like to know! Haven't we plenty to eat? Anyway, I'm friends with the fairies, and I shall go and live with *them* if you go off and leave me all alone!'

'But Beeko!' said the young cuckoos at once, 'you *must*, you really *must* come with us! No cuckoo stays in one place all the year round. You ask old Mister Blackbird or Mrs. Thrush and see!'

So Beeko asked old Mister Blackbird.

'Oho!' said Mister Blackbird, 'so you want to stay here, do you! Well, I'd like to tell you this, Master Boastful Beeko – only the strongest birds stay here for the cold winter-time, for there isn't enough food for all of us – so just you be sensible and go with the others!'

Beeko swung his tail cheekily and laughed.

'I'm strong!' he said, 'and I don't see why I shouldn't stay here if I want to, Mister Blackbird. And I'm just going to – see?'

With that he flew off as perky as could be.

He went to tell the other young cuckoos and they were really horrified. They were all getting ready to start off on their journey.

'Well, when we come back in the Springtime, we'll look for you,' they said, 'but we're very much afraid we shan't find you. You'll be dead!'

'Stuff and nonsense!' said Beeko. 'You'll find me easily enough. Just listen for an extra loud Cuckoo, Cuckoo, and you'll know it's me!'

The next night all the young cuckoos went off together. They had none of them been to the warm south lands before, but somehow they knew the way. With a great whirr and flutter of wings they were off.

'Goodbye, goodbye!' they called to Beeko, and were lost in the night.

Beeko didn't mind being left behind a bit.

'All the more food for me!' he chuckled, and ate so many grubs that he grew as fat as butter.

He very much enjoyed everyone's astonishment when they saw him.

'What!' cried a whole family of nine bluetits. 'A young cuckoo at this time of the year! Whatever can he be thinking of?'

Beeko cheekily chased them away.

'Good gracious!' cried Mrs. Jackdaw, stopping short in amazement at the sight of a cuckoo in November. 'Is it a cuckoo I see? Why, child, how is it you are silly enough to be here still?'

'How is it *you* are silly enough to be here still?' answered Beeko, rudely. 'I'm the most sensible cuckoo in the world, I am! I don't go rushing off on madcap journeys just because it's the custom to. I'm going to set a new fashion, mark my words!'

'You certainly will, you rude creature!' said Mrs. Jackdaw. 'You'll be a dead cuckoo before long. Don't you know that cuckoos and swallows and nightingales never stay here for the winter?'

Beeko didn't answer, but flew off angrily. Up till then the weather had been sunny and warm, but the nights were beginning to be rather chilly. He tried to find some fairies to cuddle up against, but to his surprise, they were all gone!

'Where have they gone to?' he asked Mister Robin, who was busily pulling a worm up from the grass.

'They've gone to Fairyland, of course!' said

Mister Robin, shortly. He didn't like Beeko at all.

'Gone to Fairyland?' said Beeko in dismay. 'But where is that? I was hoping the fairies would look after me in the winter-time!'

'Why should you think they would look after a great fellow like you?' asked Mister Robin, swallowing his worm whole. 'You ought to have gone south with the other cuckoos. I shouldn't go to Fairyland if I were you. They don't like silly disobedient birds, and they won't welcome you a bit!'

'Yes, they will, yes, they will!' cried Beeko in a fury, and flew away to find Fairyland.

But no matter how he looked, he couldn't find it. He was very upset. The days got shorter and shorter, and colder and colder. It was very difficult to find insects and grubs to eat, and Beeko grew much thinner. Mister Blackbird, Mrs. Thrush and Mister Robin wouldn't help him at all.

'There's hardly enough food for ourselves,' they said. 'It's your own fault for stopping here!'

Then one day Beeko saw a fairy in the wood! She had been to tell the primroses not to put out any little new leaves until she said so, for it was only December, and Spring was a long way off.

'Fairy, fairy!' cried Beeko. 'Take me home with you!'

'Good gracious!' cried the fairy in the greatest astonishment. It's a cuckoo! 'Have you been silly enough to stay here instead of going with the others?'

'Not *silly* enough – *clever* enough!' said Beeko, who hadn't yet learnt his lesson.

'Oh well, if that's what you think, I certainly

shan't take you home with me!' said the fairy, and flew off quickly.

Beeko followed her. She flew through the wood to the top of a hill. She stopped at a little door, hidden in the heather. She knocked three times and it opened.

Beeko watched. When she was gone, he flew down to the door and knocked three times. It opened and he flew through.

He found himself in a dark passage. He flew along for some way and at last came to a beautiful garden.

No one was there.

'Cuckoo! Cuckoo!' called Beeko, who had learnt how to cuckoo a few days before and was very proud of it.

No one came.

'CUCKOO! CUCKOO!' called Beeko, more loudly than before.

Someone came running down the path.

'Hi there! Hi there!' he called out. 'Stop that terrible noise. There's a fairy baby asleep here.'

The brownie looked so fierce that Beeko spread his wings in fright and flew away. He flew over Fairyland until he saw a dear little house set on a hill.

He flew down to it, and knocked at the door. The Balloon-Woman, whose house it was, opened the door.

'Good gracious!' she said. 'Whatever *do* you want here? A young cuckoo at this time of the year!'

'Would you take care of me and feed me?' asked Beeko. 'I can't find any food now, and it's cold.'

'Why *should* I feed you?' asked the Balloon-Woman in surprise. 'What could you do in return?'

'I couldn't do anything much,' said Beeko. 'But that wouldn't matter, would it?'

'Silly creature!' said the Balloon-Woman, and banged the door in his face.

Beeko got such a shock that he fell over backwards.

'Dear me!' he said, when he got up, 'people don't seem very kind. I must go to someone else, I suppose.'

He flew through the air, until he came to a fine palace set in a lovely garden. A grand footman came to open it.

'I want—' began Beeko.

'Please go round to the kitchen entrance,' said the footman, looking down his nose.

Beeko could hardly believe his ears. But he went.

There the Head-Cook saw him. He looked very business-like, and had his wings pinned back out of the way.

'Now then, now then!' he said. 'What do you want?'

'Please could you look after me for the winter?' asked Beeko.

The Head-Cook stared as if he couldn't believe his eyes.

'Look after a silly young cuckoo?' he cried. 'Ha! ha! Ho! ho! What a funny joke! Hi, you chaps, come and see a cuckoo who wants us to be his nurses!'

Everyone crowded round and began to laugh.

'I'll do some work if you like,' said Beeko.

'Very well,' said the Head-Cook, drying his tears of laughter. 'We want someone to clean the grates. Can you do that?'

'No,' said Beeko.

'Well, can you peel potatoes?' said the Cook.

'No,' said Beeko.

'Or pickle onions?' said the Cook.

'No,' said Beeko.

'Well then,' said the Head-Cook, exasperated, 'why didn't you go away south with the other cuckoos? Don't you know that birds as well as other people have got to earn their own livings? I suppose you thought you were clever enough to do exactly the opposite of what the other cuckoos did?'

'Yes,' said Beeko, 'b-b-but I don't now!'

'I should think *not*!' said the Cook. 'You were just silly, and now you've got to suffer for it. Go away!'

He shut the door, and Beeko was left outside. He flew off very sadly indeed, wishing and wishing he was in the warm south lands with his friends, eating fat insects all day long.

He went here and there and everywhere begging for someone to look after him, but nobody would. They all seemed to think he should do some work in return for being looked after. And poor Beeko couldn't do anything!

At last he was so hungry, thin and tired that he was nothing but a little bundle of feathers and a voice that said 'Cuckoo! Cuckoo!' He flew slowly on to the other end of Fairyland, wondering if there might be a warm land beyond.

Just at the borders of Fairyland he saw the funniest little shop. It was very small, and as Beeko flew near it he could hear a curious noise coming from it.

'Ticka – ticka – tocka – tocka – ticka – ticka – tocka – tocka!' went the noise. Beeko flew down to the door and flew in.

It was a clockmaker's shop! There were scores of clocks standing all round the walls, and on shelves and tables, ticking away, ticking away. Beeko was astonished, for he had never seen so many before.

The clockmaker sat at his table, a bent old

gnome with a very long beard and enormous spectacles. He peered over them at Beeko.

'Well?' he said. 'What do you want, little bird?'

His voice was gentle, and Beeko flew up to the table.

'I am a silly little cuckoo,' he said. 'I thought I would be clever and stay behind when the others flew away. Now I can find no food and no one will look after me. I am cold and hungry.'

'You would be in my way here,' said the clockmaker. 'I have nowhere to put you.'

'Oh, put me in a clock or anywhere!' begged Beeko.

'That's a good idea!' said the clockmaker. 'I'll make you a little cupboard above the clock I am now working on, and you shall live there!'

So he made a cupboard with a door just above the face of the clock he was making. When it was finished he hung the clock up on the wall, opened the little cupboard door above the face, and told Beeko to jump in.

In he went and the clockmaker closed the door. After a minute he opened it again.

'I am very absent-minded,' he said, 'and I might, perhaps, forget you are there. Will you pop out and cuckoo at every hour instead of the clock striking? Then I shall hear you and feed you.'

So when four o'clock came out popped Beeko and cuckooed four times. The gnome heard him and fed him. At five o'clock he cuckooed five times and was fed again, and so on all through the night, for the little gnome never slept.

There Beeko lived for many a day, warm and well-fed, loving his kind little master. He grew to know the hours so well that the gnome often put the other clocks right by his call of 'Cuckoo! Cuckoo!' and then Beeko was very proud.

Now it happened one day that the gnome went away and left his shop in charge of a goblin. A customer came in just at twelve o'clock. Out popped Beeko and called 'Cuckoo' loudly and cheerfully twelve times.

The customer's eyes nearly fell out with surprise.

'A clock that cuckoos instead of strikes!' he said. 'I'll buy it, please!'

So the clock was bought, wrapped up and taken away with poor Beeko inside. It was taken to our land and hung up in a nursery to

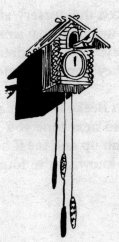

amuse the children. How they loved seeing Beeko pop out and cry 'Cuckoo! Cuckoo!'

When springtime came all the other cuckoos came back again, and the younger ones began to look for Beeko.

But they couldn't find him anywhere, until one day a bold cuckoo flew into a child's nursery and got the fright of its life when he suddenly saw a door of the clock open and a little shrunken cuckoo pop out and cry 'Cuckoo! Cuckoo!'

'It's Beeko, it's Beeko!' cried the cuckoo, and flew away to tell the others. They all came and visited the nursery and shook their heads in sorrow – and now small disobedient birds are always told the dreadful story of Beeko when they think they know better than their elders.

It is said that Beeko is still in a cuckoo-clock somewhere – so next time you hear a cuckoo in a clock, climb up and see if he is a real one. If he is, you'll know you've found Beeko.

The Tale of Twiddle and Ho

Once upon a time there lived two pixies, Twiddle and Ho. Their cottage was at the end of Hollyhock Village, and they lived there very happily together. Every day they went to work at the Pixie King's palace, not far away. It was their job to scrub the floors well, so they had to work hard, for there were many, many floors to scrub.

Twiddle and Ho got very tired of scrubbing floors, but as it was the only thing they could do really well they had to go on doing it. And then one day something happened. The Wizard Humpy came to Hollyhock Village and took the cottage next door to Twiddle and Ho.

At first the pixies were frightened, for they

knew that wizards were very clever. They
didn't even dare to peep at Humpy, who lived
quietly enough in his little cottage, and didn't
bother his neighbours at all.

Strange things happened in the wizard's cottage. Often when the kitchen fire was lit, and
the smoke came out of the chimney, it was
bright green, instead of blue-black. Another
time all the windows suddenly disappeared,
and didn't come back until night-time. The
cottage was nothing but walls and a door that
day, for bricks grew up where the windows
had been.

Then Twiddle and Ho knew that Humpy
the Wizard must have been doing very secret
magic that day, magic that he didn't want
anyone to see – so he had made all his windows vanish. It was exciting to live next door
to a wizard. You never knew what was going to
happen next. Once all the roses in the garden
began to sing a whispering song together, and
that was lovely. Another time twenty black cats
appeared from somewhere to help the wizard
in his magic, and that wasn't quite so nice
because they miaowed so very loudly.

'It's a funny thing,' said Twiddle and Ho
one day; 'it's really a very funny thing, but

Humpy the Wizard doesn't have anyone to do his housework or cooking for him. And yet his house always looks very clean and neat, doesn't it?'

'Yes,' said Ho, 'and we often smell simply LOVELY smells coming from his kitchen, even when he isn't there. I wonder what happens. Do you suppose he has a magic cat there that does things for him? Wizards and witches often have cats to help them.'

'I don't think so,' said Twiddle. 'But he might. Let's find out, shall we, Ho?'

So the two pixies kept a watch on the wizard's cottage. At first they couldn't find out anything. Then one night when it was very dark they stole out to peep into Humpy's windows for they saw that he had forgotten to draw down his blinds.

And what strange sights they saw! The wizard was sitting in a cosy arm-chair and in front of him stood a broom, a scrubbing-brush, a dish-cloth and a big yellow duster. They stood up by themselves; no one was holding them. It was very strange.

The two pixies trembled with excitement. It was wonderful to see such magic. Then they heard the wizard speaking in a deep voice.

'Broom, go and sweep,' he said. 'Scrubbing-brush, go and scrub. Dish-cloth, wash up the supper things, and mind you don't break anything. Duster, go and dust.'

All the things bowed to him, and then they started work. You should have seen them! The broom raised clouds of dust in one corner. The scrubbing-brush dipped itself in and out of a pail of soapy water and scrubbed the floor till it shone beautifully.

The dish-cloth flew to the sink and began to wash up the wizard's dirty plates and dishes.

It was wonderful to see it. As for the duster, it did its work really well, and even remembered to dust the tops of the pictures, a place that Twiddle and Ho always forgot when *they* dusted!

Suddenly Humpy the Wizard lifted his head and began to sniff as if he smelt something unusual. Twiddle and Ho crept quickly back to their cottage, for they guessed that he could smell pixies, and would come and look for them if they didn't go.

They looked at one another, as they sat sipping hot cocoa before going to bed.

'What strange things we have seen, Ho,' said Twiddle.

'We have indeed, Twiddle,' said Ho. 'No wonder Humpy's house always looking spotless, if he has such willing servants! I wish *we* had some like them!'

Now two days after that the wizard shut his house up and went away. He didn't say where he was going nor how long he would be gone. He just went.

Twiddle and Ho thought of something. They both thought of the same thing, but for a long time they didn't like to say it to one another. At last Twiddle whispered it to Ho.

'Ho,' he said, 'do you suppose we could borrow the wizard's scrubbing-brush until Humpy comes back? If we did, it would scrub the palace floors for us and we could have a nice rest. We could go and sit under the plum trees in the palace gardens and listen to the birds whilst the scrubbing-brush did all our work for us!'

'That's just what I've been thinking, too,' said Ho, delighted. 'Let's!'

So that night the two naughty pixies crept into the wizard's back garden, and opened the kitchen window. Twiddle slipped in and felt all round for the scrubbing-brush. They didn't want anything else – only the brush.

At last he found it. It was a big brush, heavy and strong, just the sort for scrubbing wide palace floors. Twiddle was shaking with excitement when he climbed out of the window. He gave the brush to Ho to hold, and then carefully shut the window again.

Back home they went, carrying the brush. They looked at it by the light of their candle, but except that its bristles were bright blue, it seemed just the same as any other scrubbing-brush. They put it in a pail by the sink for the night and then went to bed.

In the morning they carried the brush to the palace and told the cook there that for once they would use their own brush, which was a very wonderful one. So the cook simply gave them their pail of soapy water and didn't bother about scrubbing-brushes.

'You're to scrub the big hall this morning, and then the King's own bedroom,' said the cook. So off went Twiddle and Ho to the big hall. They set the brush on the floor and spoke to it.

'Scrubbing-brush, go and scrub!' they said. 'First this big hall and then the King's own bedroom.'

To their great delight the brush at once dipped itself in the soapy water and then began to scrub the floor. You should have seen how hard it worked! The pixies stood and watched in amazement. How pleased the King would be when he saw how well his floors had been scrubbed that day!

'Now we'll go and have a nice sit-down in the garden under the plum trees,' said Twiddle. So off they went. At first they listened to the birds, but soon the hot sun made them drowsy and they nodded their small heads and fell fast asleep.

In the palace, the scrubbing-brush was working hard. It scrubbed the whole of the floor of the big hall, and then it obediently went upstairs, taking the pail with it, to the King's bedroom. The carpets had been taken up ready for the floor to be scrubbed.

The brush began its work. How it scrubbed! It went into every corner and made them as clean as could be. It wasn't very long before it had finished. It sat in the pail for a few minutes, and then hopped out again. It seemed to look around for a moment or two, and then it hopped to the King's bed.

On the bed was spread a beautiful eiderdown of silver and gold, with shining flowers made of diamonds here and there. The brush began to scrub it! Dear me, what a mess it made of that fine eiderdown! The soapy water was very dirty, and very soon the eiderdown was dirty, too. The brush was rough and scrubbed off many of the shining diamond flowers. Then, when it had done all it could, it looked around again.

It thought it would scrub the ceiling! Up it went and scrubbed so hard that all the lamps fell off the ceiling. Then it scrubbed the walls, and down went the pictures, crash, onto the

floor. The brush was quite mad with joy. It liked scrubbing when it could make things fall down and break. It was exciting.

The butler heard the noise and came running to see what it was. When he saw what was happening he was amazed! He watched the brush try to scrub a vase of flowers and break the glass to bits. Then he rushed over to the brush and tried to catch hold of it.

The brush rose up and hit him on the head. Crack! The butler took a step backwards and cried out in pain. The brush made a noise that sounded like a chuckle and began to scrub off all the things on the King's dressing-table. They flew to the floor and broke. The butler gave a loud cry of fright and rushed to the kitchen. Soon the cook came back with him and stared open-mouthed at what was happening.

'It's the magic brush those two pixies brought with them this morning!' she cried. 'The little rascals! They have left the brush to do their work and instead of staying to look after it they have gone to sit in the garden!'

The butler went to fetch Twiddle and Ho. He found them under the plum trees, fast asleep. How he shook them!

They woke with a dreadful jump, and when they heard what the butler had to say, they turned quite pale. They rushed into the palace and went to the King's bedroom. There they saw what a dreadful mess it was in, lamps, pictures and everything else on the floor, and the brush trying to scrub the bottle of medicine that the King took three times a day.

Twiddle and Ho rushed at the brush and tried to pick it up. Rap! Crack! Twiddle got a sharp rap on his knuckles, and Ho got a blow on the head. And no matter how hard they

tried to get hold of that brush they couldn't –
it simply hit them hard and hopped away.

'Can't you stop it scrubbing?' shouted the
butler, angrily. 'You started it off, didn't you
– well, stop it, then!'

'Stop scrubbing!' cried Twiddle and Ho.
But the brush took no notice at all. Then
the pixies felt dreadful. They remembered that
they hadn't heard what the wizard said to stop
the brush from scrubbing, because they had
crept back home before the work had been
finished.

Suddenly a voice behind them made them
jump in fright. It was the King, returned home
from his ride.

'What's all this?' he asked in astonishment.
'Why are you all in my bedroom? And what a
dreadful mess it is in!'

The butler explained what had happened –
but before he had finished, the brush hopped
over the floor to the King and began to scrub
his boots! Then it flew to his head and began
to scrub his hair!

The King was angry, and as for the two
pixies, they trembled with fright. How dare
the brush scrub the King himself!

The King knew a good deal of magic. He

called out a few words and the brush left him. It rushed to Twiddle and Ho and began to scrub *them*! How they yelled!

'Go home and take your brush with you!' said the King sternly. 'And don't come here again. You have lost your job.'

Crying bitterly the two pixies left the palace – and the brush went with them. It scrubbed them hard all the way home, and poor Twiddle had no tunic left when at last he went into his cottage. What were they to do? They didn't know *how* to stop the brush!

'If only the Wizard Humpy would come home, we could go and confess and ask him to take away this hateful brush,' sobbed

Twiddle. But there was no one in the wizard's cottage. He hadn't come back. So all that night Twiddle and Ho had to put up with the brush scrubbing them hard, and it was very painful indeed.

Next morning, to their great joy, they saw Humpy the Wizard going into his cottage. He had come back!

At once they rushed into his garden and knocked at the door, the brush scrubbing away at their shoes all the time. Humpy opened the door and when he saw what was happening he *did* look surprised.

Twiddle and Ho told him everything.

'We are very, very sorry for what we did,' they said. 'Please forgive us and take away your scrubbing-brush.'

'I don't want it,' said Humpy. 'It's never been a really good one. I can get another. You can keep that, seeing you borrowed it.'

'But we don't want it!' cried Twiddle, in a panic. 'We don't want it, Humpy. We hate it! It has spoilt all our clothes with its horrid scrubbing, and besides it is so painful to be scrubbed all day. Do take it away.'

'No, I don't want it,' said Humpy. 'It serves you right for borrowing without asking.'

'Oh, we'll do anything for you if only you'll take away this horrid brush,' sobbed Ho.

'Well,' said Humpy, 'I'll make a bargain with you. I can sell my magic broom, scrubbing-brush, dish-cloth and duster to Green-eye the witch. But if I do that I shan't have anything to do my housework for me, and nobody will be servant to a wizard if they can help it. Will you come and do all my housework for me, if I take away that brush?'

'Oh, yes, yes!' cried the pixies.

So the wizard clapped his hands three times and cried: 'Brush! Go to your pail!' At once the brush left the pixies and flew to a pail

under the sink, where it stayed quite quietly. How glad the pixies were!

But now they are the wizard's servants and they have to work twice as hard as they used to do. They sweep and scrub, mop and dust from morning till night, and they are very very glad to creep home and sit down to a cup of hot cocoa before going to bed. Then they look at one another and shake their heads.

'We won't take anything that doesn't belong to us EVER again!' says Twiddle. And I don't suppose they ever will!

The Wishing Carpet

Once upon a time there were two children who owned a wishing carpet. A little old woman had given it to them in exchange for a basket of mushrooms. They had met her on Breezy Hill when they were gathering mushrooms, and she had begged them to give her their basketful.

'Here you are, my dears,' she said, when they handed her their mushrooms. 'Here is something in exchange for your mushrooms. It is a magic carpet. Take great care of it.'

They took it home and unrolled it. It was bright blue and yellow, with a magic word written in green round the border. Peter and Betty looked at the carpet in wonder.

'I say!' said Peter. 'Suppose it really *is*

magic, Betty! Shall we sit on it and wish ourselves somewhere else and see what happens?'

'Yes,' said Betty. So they sat themselves down on it, and Peter wished.

'Take us to the big city of London,' he said. The carpet didn't move. Peter spoke again.

'I said take us to the big city of London,' he said, more loudly. Still the carpet didn't move. It was most disappointing. And no matter what the two children did or said it just lay still on the floor and behaved like any ordinary carpet.

'It *isn't* a wishing carpet, after all!' said Betty, disappointed. 'That old woman wasn't telling the truth.'

'What a shame!' said Peter. 'Let's roll it up and put it in our toy-cupboard. We won't tell the grown-ups about it because they might laugh at us for believing the old woman.'

So they rolled it up and put it right at the back of the toy-cupboard. They forgot all about it until about four weeks later when they met a very strange-looking little man in their garden.

'What are you doing here?' demanded Peter.

'Sh!' said the little man. 'I'm a gnome. I've

come to speak to you about that magic carpet of yours.'

'It isn't a magic carpet at all,' said Peter. 'It's just a fraud. It won't take us anywhere.'

'Show it to me and I'll tell you how to make it take you wherever you want to go!' said the gnome eagerly.

'Come on, then,' said Peter, and he led the way indoors. But on the way Betty pulled at his sleeve.

'I don't like that little gnome at all,' she said. 'I'm sure he is a bad gnome, Peter. I don't think we'd better show him the carpet. He might want to steal it.'

'Don't be afraid,' said Peter. 'I shall have tight hold of it all the time!'

He led the way to the toy-cupboard and pulled out the carpet. He laid it on the floor and then sat on it. The gnome clapped his hands in joy when he saw it and sat down too.

'Come on, Betty,' said Peter. 'Come and sit down as well. This may be an adventure. Oh look, here's Bonzo, the puppy. He wants to come as well! Come on, Bonzo, sit down on the carpet too.'

So Betty and Bonzo sat down beside the gnome and Peter.

'Did you say the magic word that is written round the border of the carpet?' asked the gnome.

'Oh, no!' said Peter. 'I didn't know I had to.'

'Well, no wonder the carpet wouldn't move then!' said the gnome. 'Listen!'

He looked closely at the word round the carpet border, and then clapped his hands twice.

'Arra-gitty-borra-ba!' he said. 'Take us to Fairyland!'

In a trice the carpet trembled throughout its length, and then rose in the air. It flew out of the window and rose as high as the chimney-pots. The children gasped in astonishment and held on tightly, afraid of falling off. The carpet flew steadily westwards.

'Oh!' said Peter. 'So that's how you do it! My goodness, what an adventure! Are we really going to Fairyland?'

'Yes,' said the gnome. 'Keep a watch out to the west. You will soon see the towers and pinnacles on the borders.'

Sure enough, it was not long before the children saw shimmering towers and high-flung pinnacles far away on the blue horizon.

The carpet flew at a great speed, and the world below seemed to flow away from them like a river, so fast were they going.

'Fairyland!' cried Betty. 'Oh how lovely!'

They soon passed over a high wall, and then the carpet rapidly flew downwards to a big square that seemed to be used for a market. And then something dreadful happened.

The carpet had hardly reached the ground when the gnome gave Peter a hard push that sent him rolling off the carpet. Bonzo rolled off too – but Betty was still on it with the gnome.

'Ha ha!' cried the gnome. 'I'm off with

Betty! She shall be my servant! I've got the carpet for my own, foolish boy! Arra-gitty-borra-ba! Take me to my castle, carpet!'

Before Peter or Bonzo could pick themselves up and rush to reach the carpet, it had once more risen in the air and was flying high above the chimney tops. Peter groaned in despair.

'Oh dear, oh dear, whatever shall I do? Betty felt certain that that gnome was a bad old fellow, and I didn't take any notice of her. Now he will make her his servant and perhaps I'll never see her again!'

Bonzo put his nose into Peter's hand, and much to the little boy's surprise, he spoke.

'Don't worry, Peter,' he said. 'I expect we'll get her back again all right.'

'Good gracious, you can speak!' cried Peter in surprise.

'Well, we're in Fairyland, you see,' said Bonzo. 'All animals can speak here.'

Peter looked round the market square. He saw many pixies, elves and brownies looking at him, and he went up to some of them.

'Could you please help me?' he asked. 'My little sister has been taken away on my magic carpet by a horrid little gnome. I don't know where he's gone to, but I really *must* get Betty back again. She will be so frightened all by herself.'

'How dreadful!' cried the fairy folk. 'Why, that must have been Sly-One! He lives in a castle far away from here. Nobody dares to go near him because he is so powerful.'

'Well, I must go and find him,' said Peter bravely. 'I've got to rescue my sister. Tell me how to get to Sly-One's castle.'

'The Blue Bird will take you to the land where he lives,' said a pixie. 'There you will find an old dame in a yellow cottage, and she will tell you which way to go next.'

'Oh, thank you,' said Peter. 'Where can I find the Blue Bird?'

'We'll get him for you,' said the little folk. One of them took out a silver whistle from his pocket, and blew seven blasts on it. In a few moments there came the sound of flapping wings and a great blue bird soared over the market place. It flew down among the little folk and they ran to it.

'Blue Bird, we want your help,' they cried. 'Will you take this boy to the Land of Higgledy, where Sly-One the Gnome lives? His sister has been carried off there and he wants to rescue her.'

'Certainly,' said the bird. 'Jump on.'

So Peter and Bonzo climbed up on the Blue Bird's soft, feathery back. He spread his broad wings, and flew off into the air. Peter held tight, and Bonzo whined, for he was rather frightened.

'It's a good way off,' said the Blue Bird. 'It will take quite half an hour to get there. Feel about behind my neck and you'll find a box of chocolate biscuits. You may help yourself.'

Peter did as he was told. He soon found the box and opened it. Inside was the finest collection of chocolate biscuits he had ever tasted, and he did wish Betty could have shared them. He gave Bonzo three, and the little dog crunched them all up.

In half an hour's time the Blue Bird turned his head round once more and spoke to Peter.

'We're nearly there,' he said. 'Can you see some of the houses?'

Peter looked down. He saw a very curious land. All the trees and houses were higgledy-piggledy. The trees grew twisted and crooked, the houses were built in crooked rows, and

their windows and chimneys were set higgledy-piggledy anywhere.

The bird flew down to the ground, and
Peter and Bonzo got off his back.

'Thank you very much,' said Peter. 'It was
very good of you to help me.'

'Don't mention it,' said the Blue Bird. 'Take
one of my feathers, little boy, and put it into
your pocket. It may be useful to you, for when-
ever you want to know where anything is it
will at once point in the right direction.'

'Oh, thank you,' said Peter, and he pulled a

little blue feather from the bird's neck. He put it into his pocket, said goodbye, and then looked about for the yellow cottage that the little folk had told him about.

It was just a little way off, standing by the side of a lane. It was all crooked, and looked as if it might tumble down at any moment. An old woman stood at the gate, knitting. Peter went up to her.

'Please,' he said, 'could you tell me the way to the castle of Sly-One the Gnome.'

'I should advise you not to go there,' said the old dame, knitting very fast indeed. 'He is a bad lot, that gnome.'

'I know,' said Peter. 'But he's got my sister, so I'm afraid I *must* go to him.'

'Dear, dear, is that so?' said the old woman. 'Well, little boy, catch the bus at the end of the lane, and ask for Cuckoo Corner. Get off there, and look for a green mushroom behind the hedge. Sit on it and wish yourself underground. As soon as you find yourself in the earth, call for Mister Mole. He will tell you what to do next.'

'Thank you,' said Peter. Then, hearing the rumbling sound of a bus, he ran up the lane. At the top he saw a wooden bus drawn by rabbits. He got in, sat down on a seat with Bonzo at his feet, and waited for the conductor to give him a ticket. The conductor was a duck, and he asked Peter where he wanted to go.

'Cuckoo Corner,' said Peter. 'How much, please?'

'Bless you, we don't charge anything on this bus,' said the duck, giving Peter a ticket as large as a post card. 'I'll tell you when we get to Cuckoo Corner.'

But Peter didn't need to be told – for at Cuckoo Corner there was a most tremendous noise of cuckoos cuckooing for all they were worth! Peter hopped out of the bus, and looked for the green mushroom behind the hedge. He soon found it and thought it looked very peculiar.

'I've never seen a green mushroom before,' he said to Bonzo. 'Come on, puppy. Jump on my knee, or you may get left behind!'

He sat down on the mushroom and wished himself underground. Bonzo gave a bark of fright as he felt himself sinking downwards, and Peter lost all his breath. Down they went, and down. Then bump! They came to rest in a cave far underground. It was lit by

glow-worms who sat in little lamps all about the cave. Peter jumped off the mushroom.

'Now, where's Mister Mole?' he thought. He looked around but could see no one.

'Mister Mole!' he shouted. 'Mister Mole! Where are you?'

'Wuff! Mister Mole!' Bonzo shouted too.

Suddenly a door opened in the wall of the cave and a mole with spectacles on his nose looked into the cave.

'Here I am,' he said. 'What do you want?'

'Please will you help me?' said Peter. 'I

want to rescue my sister from Sly-One the Gnome and I don't know what to do next.'

'Well, this door leads to the cellars of Sly-One's castle,' said the mole. 'Come with me.'

Peter followed the mole through the door, and found himself in a large cellar which seemed never-ending. Boxes and bottles stood all about, and except for the glow-worms in lamps, the place was quite dark.

The mole led him to some steps.

'If you go up there you'll come to the gnome's kitchen,' he said. 'Go quietly, because there is someone there. You can hear footsteps on the floor above, if you listen.'

Peter listened, and sure enough he heard someone walking about overhead. He felt rather frightened. Suppose it should be the gnome?

He went quietly up the steps – and then, oh dear! Bonzo suddenly gave a whine and darted right up them, ahead of Peter. He disappeared through a door at the top, and Peter was left alone. He looked upwards in dismay.

'How stupid of Bonzo!' he thought. 'If that was the gnome, he'll be warned, and will be waiting for me at the top! Well, I can't help it! Here goes!'

Quietly he climbed the rest of the steps, and came to the door, which was half open. He listened, and thought that he heard someone crying. He popped his head suddenly round the door – and, oh my, whoever should he see but Betty herself in a large kitchen, crying and laughing over Bonzo, who was licking her face in excitement.

'Betty!' cried Peter, and he ran to her and hugged her. How glad she was to see him!

'That horrid gnome brought me to his castle and took me to this kitchen,' said Betty. 'He says I'm to scrub the floor and cook his dinner. Oh, Peter, how can we escape from here?'

'I'll find a way!' said Peter, bravely – but just as he said that, his heart sank almost into his boots, for who should come stamping into the kitchen at that very moment but the horrid gnome himself!

'Ha!' he said in surprise, when he saw Peter. 'So you think you'll rescue your sister, do you? Well, you're mistaken. There are no doors to this castle, and only one window, which is right at the very top! You can't get out of there! As for this cellar door which you came here by, I'll lock it this very instant! Now I shall have two servants instead of one! Well, you can start work at once. Scrub the floor, please.'

Peter watched him in dismay. He locked the cellar door with a large key, pulled Betty's hair, boxed Peter on the ears, and then went out of the kitchen, whistling.

Betty began to cry again.

'Don't be frightened,' said Peter. 'There must be some way out!'

He looked around the kitchen. It had no window, and no door led outside. He ran into the hall. That had no door and no window either. There was another room opposite, and Peter looked into it. It was no use – there wasn't a single door that led outside, and not a window to be seen. The rooms were all lit by candles.

The gnome came into the kitchen again and when he saw that Peter and Betty had done nothing, he fell into a rage.

'Now set to work!' he cried. 'If my dinner isn't ready in ten minutes, I'll turn you both into beetles. Fry me some bacon and eggs, make me some tea, and toast me some bread!'

He stamped out of the kitchen and left the children in a panic. Neither knew how to fry

bacon and eggs. But Bonzo came to the rescue.

'I've often watched Cook,' he said. 'I'll do the bacon and eggs, if you'll make the tea and the toast.'

So all three set to work, and soon the gnome's meal was ready on a tray. Peter took the tray in his hands and went into the hall. The gnome looked over the banisters of the staircase, and told him to bring it up to him. Peter carried it up and the gnome led the way to a tiny room whose walls were lined all round with big magic books.

He set the tray on the table and then ran down to Betty again.

'If we're going to escape, we'd better do it now!' he said. 'The gnome's busy eating.'

'But how can we get away?' asked Betty. 'There's no way we can go.'

'If only we knew where the magic carpet was!' said Peter.

'I say!' Bonzo suddenly cried. 'What about that feather the Blue Bird gave you, Peter? Can't you use that to find the carpet?'

'Of course!' cried Peter and he took the feather from his pocket. He held it up in the air, and spoke to it. 'Point to where the magic carpet is!' he commanded. At once the feather twisted round in Peter's hand and pointed towards the door that led into the hall.

'Come on,' said Peter. 'It will show us the way!'

They all went into the hall. Then the feather pointed up the stairs. So up they all went, keeping as quiet as they could in case the gnome heard them. Past the door where he was eating his meal they went, and up more stairs. Still the feather pointed upwards. So up they went. At last they came to a broad landing, and on it stood a big chest. The blue feather pointed to it.

Betty ran to the chest and opened it. Inside lay the magic carpet. With a cry of joy she unrolled it and laid it on the floor. And at that very moment the gnome came rushing up the stairs.

'Ho!' he cried. 'So that is what you're doing!'

'Quick, quick!' cried Peter, pulling Betty on to the carpet. The gnome rushed up to them – and then brave Bonzo rushed at the gnome, growling fiercely.

'Keep back or I'll bite you!' he said.

The gnome crouched back against the wall, frightened.

'Bonzo, Bonzo, come on to the carpet!' cried Peter. 'We must go whilst we can!'

'I can't!' said Bonzo. 'I must keep the gnome safely in a corner whilst you go. Never mind me.'

So Peter spoke the magic word, though he was dreadfully sorry to leave brave Bonzo behind – but he knew that he must rescue Betty whilst he could.

'Arra-gitty-borra-ba!' he cried. 'Take us home again!'

At once the carpet rose from the ground and flew upwards. It went up staircase after staircase, for the castle was very tall. At last it came to a big open window right at the very top and flew out. And just then Peter heard Bonzo barking, and caught the sound of his feet tearing up the stairs.

'Wait, wait!' he said to the carpet. 'Wait for Bonzo!' But the carpet didn't wait. It flew right out of the window and began to sail away to the east. Peter was in despair.

Bonzo appeared at the window – and, oh my, whatever do you think he did? He saw the carpet sailing away and he jumped! It was a most tremendous jump, and he nearly missed the carpet! As it was, he wouldn't have got there safely if Peter hadn't caught his tail, and pulled him on.

'Oh dear, oh dear!' said Betty, the tears pouring down her cheeks. 'I really thought we had lost you, dear Bonzo, darling Bonzo!'

She hugged him and hugged him and so did Peter.

'You are the bravest puppy I ever knew,' said Peter. 'Did you bite the gnome?'

'Yes, I did,' said Bonzo. 'He tried to get past me to go after you, so I bit his ankle. He cried

out in rage and ran down the stairs to get a
bandage. So I tore up the stairs to try and
catch you up.'

How happy they all were to be going home
together! They passed right over Fairyland,
and soon, came to their own land. It was not
long before they were over their own garden,
and the carpet flew down to their nursery
window. In a moment they all got off, and
danced around in delight.

'Bonzo, can you still talk?' asked Betty.

'Wuff, wuff, wuff, wuff!' said Bonzo.

'Oh, you can't!' said Peter. 'But never mind,

we understand your barks. Now what shall we do with the magic carpet?'

'If we keep it I'm sure the nasty gnome will come after it again,' said Betty. 'Let's send it away in the air by itself! *We* shan't want to use it again after all our adventures, I'm sure.'

'All right,' said Peter. He spoke to the carpet.

'Arra-gitty-borra-ba!' he said. 'Rise up in the air and fly round and round the world!'

At once the carpet rose and flew out of the window. It was soon out of sight, and the children sighed with relief.

'That's the end of *that*!' they said. 'What an adventure! Let's go and tell Mummy all about it!'

The Children Who Wouldn't Go To Bed

There were once two children, Pat and Janet, who wouldn't go to bed when they were told. At seven o'clock their mother would say:

'Now, Pat; now, Janet! Stop your playing and go up to bed like good children!'

'Oh, Mother, just let's finish our game!' Pat would say, and he would go on building with his bricks, or drawing in his book.

And Janet would say: 'Oh, Mother, let me finish what I'm doing!'

Then, of course, they would go on and on playing until Mother would call again, and at last she would have to take them up to bed herself. That made her cross, because she had Baby to look after too, and she did expect the big ones to help and obey her.

Now one evening, the children were out in the garden, playing at 'Touch-Me-Last'. Mother called them as usual.

'Time for bed, dears! Come along in and go upstairs, there's good children!'

'Oh, just a few minutes more!' cried Pat, and he ran down the garden to catch Janet. She slipped through a hole in the hedge and Pat went after her – and do you know, it was a most extraordinary thing, but just the other side of the hedge was a small yellow and red bus! It was full of children, and they called to Pat and Janet.

'Come on, come on!'

Pat and Janet ran up to the bus to see what it was like. There was a strange conductor on the back step of the bus and when the children came near, he took hold of their hands and pulled them into the bus. They fell over the feet of all the other children, and then looked around in surprise.

The bus started off. It was quite full.

'Where are we going?' asked Janet. 'And what is this funny little bus? I've never seen it before!'

'Oh, it's the bus that takes off the Children Who Don't Want to Go to Bed!' said the conductor. 'It's a shame for children to have to go to bed if they don't want to. So I and the driver run this bus about and pick up those children who are still playing, and take them off to Playtime Hall to play as long as they like!'

'Oh, fancy!' said Janet, in surprise. 'How nice!'

'Can we really play as long as we like there?' asked Pat.

'Oh yes,' said the conductor, giving Pat and Janet two large yellow tickets, with Playtime Hall printed on them. 'You will play all night long!'

'What fun!' cried all the children in glee, and they drummed their feet on the floor and longed to get to Playtime Hall.

At last they arrived. It was more like a palace than a hall. There were lights shining in it from top to bottom and it was gaily decorated with flags and lanterns. The children were most excited. They jumped out of the bus and ran into Playtime Hall.

At the door stood three round, fat little men to welcome the children and see to the games.

'First of all we'll have "Musical Chairs"!' they cried. So they began. They played and played and played, and at last some of the children began to feel rather tired. But the little fat men wouldn't let them sit down for long. Oh no, they had to join in another game. This time it was 'Puss in the Corner' and that game lasted for a long time, too. Pat and Janet got tired of it and suddenly they thought they would watch instead of playing.

So they went to sit down – but the little fat men ran up to them in great surprise and pulled them back into the game again.

'You *must* play!' they cried. 'You *must* play! You've come here to play, haven't you? You wanted to play instead of going to bed, didn't you? Well, then you *must* play!'

So Pat and Janet *had* to play! There was no help for it. The next game was 'Hunt the

Slipper' and Janet was the one trying to get the shoe from the others. She tried and tried, but she couldn't. They were too sharp for her.

'I give it up!' she said, at last. 'I feel tired. I'll sit down and someone else must be the one to find the shoe.'

But that wouldn't do at all! Oh no! One of the little fat men came up and scolded her for being lazy and Janet felt like crying.

'I'm not lazy, I'm only rather tired,' she said. 'After all, it's long past my bedtime!'

'Sh! Sh! Bedtime is never mentioned here!' cried the little man, in horror. 'We never go to bed here! Bed is a shame! It's a pity people ever have to go to bed!'

'Are we going to play all night, then?' asked Pat.

'Of course,' said the fat little man, rubbing his hands together in glee. 'The next game will be "Gathering Nuts and May"!'

They played 'Nuts and May' for ages. Then they played 'Touch-Me-Last', and then they played 'Ring-a-Ring-of-Roses', which Pat and Janet and most of the others thought a very babyish game. They had to fall down so often that Pat got quite tired of it. He sat down plop and stayed there! He wouldn't get up for the next ring.

The little fat men scolded him and pulled him to his feet.

'You *must* play!' they said. 'You *must* play! We brought you here to play instead of going to bed.'

'Well, I wish I *was* in bed,' said a little girl, yawning. 'I feel awfully sleepy. It must be about ten o'clock. I've never been up so late before. Oh, I wish I was in bed.'

One of the little men ran up to her and smacked her sharply.

'You ungrateful child!' he said. 'Don't let me hear you mention bed in Playtime Hall. You've come here to PLAY, and PLAY you shall!'

The next game was 'Here we go round the Mulberry Bush'. It was very tiring. All the children were yawning by the end of it, and Janet felt as if she could go to sleep standing on her feet. She was very tired of playing. She wished and wished she had gone in to bed when Mother had called her that evening.

At the end of the next game, which was 'Blind Man's Buff', two children fell asleep. But the little men shook them hard and woke

them up. They threw cups of cold water in the poor children's faces to wake them up properly, and that made the children very cross.

'I want to go home!' wailed one little girl. 'I want to go home and go to bed!'

'You must PLAY!' said a little man, bustling up. 'You said you didn't want to go to bed, when your mother told you to – you said you would like to play all night. You don't know your own mind, chopping and changing about like that. Play! Hurry up now – PLAY!'

Once again the children played, this time 'Twos and Threes'. Just as they were finishing, a clock struck twelve. Dong – dong – dong – twelve times!

'Ooh! It's midnight!' said Pat to Janet. 'Ooh!

Isn't it dreadfully late! Mummy and Daddy and everyone will be in bed now!'

'Sh! Sh!' cried the little men, whilst the clock went on striking. As it struck the last stroke, all the lights in Playtime Hall went out, and there was darkness and silence everywhere. Pat put out his hand and felt Janet's. They waited for the lights to go on. But they didn't!

Pat groped about to find where he was – and his hands touched something soft – it felt just like a bed! Then he found a candle on a little table by the bed and he lighted it.

What a very strange and peculiar thing! He and Janet were in their own night nursery at home! There was Janet's bed in the corner over there, and here was his! How had they managed to get back into the nursery? When the lights had gone out they had been in Playtime Hall!

'I'm so sleepy I'm going to drag my clothes off and get into bed,' said Janet. And she did. In two minutes she was asleep and so was Pat.

Mother didn't seem to know that anything had happened when they saw her next morning – but that evening at seven o'clock she *was* surprised to see the children come running to her.

'I haven't called you for bed yet,' she said. 'I was going to give you a few minutes longer.'

'It's all right, Mummy, we'll go right up to bed now,' said Pat, kissing her. 'We're always going to bed when it's time, every night, without you telling us. We think it's silly to go on playing after bedtime.'

Mother *was* astonished, and she wondered whatever could have happened to change the children so. She doesn't know even now why they are always so good at bedtime – but I do, don't you? They don't want to have to catch the Playtime Bus again – and I'm sure *I* don't want to, either!

The Magic Egg

There was once a little pixie called Pickle, and his name was really just right for him. He *was* a pickle! He was into mischief here, there and everywhere, and his house and garden were always in a pickle too, for they were dreadfully dirty and untidy.

But Pickle didn't care! So long as there was something to eat in the larder, and his morning newspaper came at ten o'clock to the tick, he was happy. He got up very late each day, boiled himself an egg, took up his newspaper from the front door-mat and then sat down to enjoy himself.

One morning, when he looked into the larder, he found that there wasn't a single egg left! He had had the last one the day before.

'Bother!' said Pickle. 'And I haven't a penny to buy one with today! Now what am I to do? I'm not going to go without my breakfast!'

Just then he heard a great cackling from next door, and he peeped out of the window. He saw Dame Bollo's hens there, and, by the loud cackling, he guessed that one of them had laid an egg.

Nobody was about. Dame Bollo had already gone out shopping. As he stood and looked at the hens, a naughty thought came into Pickle's mind. Should he go and see if there was an egg? If there was, he would take it and have it for his breakfast.

He slipped out, climbed over the wall and ran to the hen-house – and there, in the very first nest, was a big egg! Pickle picked it up, climbed back into his garden and ran indoors. Then he got a saucepan to boil some water for the egg.

It was rather a funny egg. It had stripes of pale pink all down it. Pickle had never seen one like it before.

'But it will taste just the same inside!' he thought, and popped it into the saucepan. It was soon boiled, and he put it into his blue egg-cup. Then he picked up his paper from

the mat, and sat down to enjoy his breakfast
and his reading.

He cracked the egg. Fuff! Out came a
stream of pink smoke, and a strange squeaking
noise! Pickle stared in surprise. Whatever was
the matter with the egg?

The smoke faded away, and something
began to climb out of the egg. Pickle looked
in horror. It was a little imp, dressed in a tight-
fitting tunic striped in pale pink!

'What are you doing in my egg?' cried the
pixie. 'Why aren't you a proper egg?'

The imp took no notice. He climbed right

out of the egg, and then sat down on a salt-cellar. He looked at Pickle, and still said nothing.

Then Pickle noticed that the imp was growing fast. He was soon too big for the salt-cellar, so he sat on the toast-rack. But it wasn't very long before he was too big for that too, and so he sat on the loaf of bread.

'Whatever do you think you are doing?' asked Pickle, crossly. 'Get off my breakfast table.'

The imp jumped off, and stood on a chair – and will you believe it, very soon he was as big as the pixie himself – and then even bigger!

'My goodness!' said Pickle, getting quite frightened. 'When do you stop growing?'

'Now!' said the imp, and so he did! He took up the pixie's newspaper, sat down in the comfortable armchair, and opened the paper.

'Well!' cried the pixie, in a rage. 'What rudeness! Give me my paper at once, and go away next door, where you belong!'

'Don't be impolite to me,' said the imp. 'If you are, I shall tell Dame Bollo that you stole her magic egg, and then you will be sent to prison.'

Pickle turned very pale. He knew that Dame

Bollo was a cross, impatient person, quite likely to fetch a policeman if she knew that one of her precious eggs had been stolen. He looked at the imp, and wondered what to say next.

'If you've finished your breakfast, please clear away,' said the imp. 'If there's one thing I do hate, it's seeing dirty dishes in front of me!'

'Clear them away yourself,' said the pixie, rudely.

'If you can't be polite to me, I shall fight you,' said the imp. 'I'm bigger than you, so I would win. You'd better be careful.'

Pickle looked at the imp, and decided that he had better clear away the dishes. He put them all into the sink and left them there.

'Please wash them up,' said the imp. 'Surely you're not going to leave them there! And what about your bed? I may want to sleep in it tonight, so please put clean sheets on, and make it properly. It looks as if it hasn't been made for days! And what about washing your kitchen floor and cleaning the windows? I never saw such a dirty house in my life!'

'You be quiet!' said Pickle, fiercely. 'And you can wash up and scrub the floor yourself if you want to. As to sleeping in my bed, well, you jolly well won't!'

'Then I suppose I must go back to Dame Bollo and tell her how I came to be hatched before my time,' said the imp, folding up the newspaper.

Pickle turned pale again. He didn't want Dame Bollo to know that he had taken one of her eggs. He really didn't know what she would do to him if she knew!

'No, don't do that,' he said. 'You can stay with me, if you like. It's much nicer here than next door. Dame Bollo has such a bad temper.'

'Well, I don't mind staying with you, if you'll get things a bit cleaner,' said the imp. 'But really, you know, I couldn't possibly make myself at home in a house as dirty as this!'

'I'll clean it up nicely,' promised the pixie, and he began straightaway. He washed up the dishes, scrubbed the floor, made the bed, cleaned the windows, went out shopping and brought back a nice joint of meat to cook. He had promised the butcher to go and wash his shop for him each day for a week in return for the meat.

The imp said the curtains were dirty, so Pickle washed those too. He took the carpet

out of doors and beat all the dust out of it. He cooked a beautiful dinner and made some lemonade.

He and the imp sat down to the roast meat and enjoyed it very much. The imp was quite nice to Pickle for a wonder, and said that the pixie could have the paper to look at, when he had washed everything up.

The imp didn't offer to help at all. He just sat and lazed whilst Pickle did all the hard work. The pixie was so tired that night that he could hardly keep awake.

The imp crept in between the nice clean sheets on the pixie's bed, and was soon asleep. There was nowhere for Pickle to sleep, except the mat before the fire. He curled up on that, and soon fell asleep too.

Early in the morning the imp woke up and called Pickle.

'I want an early cup of tea,' he said. 'Make haste!'

Poor Pickle jumped to his feet, and put the kettle on to boil, after he had lit the fire. The imp grumbled all the time because he was so long in bringing the cup of tea.

Pickle worked hard that day and the next. There was no pleasing that imp – and what a lot he ate! Pickle was always buying food to eat. His cottage was soon as clean and neat as a pin, and then the imp made him dig up his garden and weed it. The meals had to be punctual, and each night the imp slept in Pickle's cosy bed.

At last the pixie felt that he really couldn't put up with the imp any longer, he was so expensive. He was so rude and unkind too.

'I shall go next door to Dame Bollo and tell her what I did,' he thought. 'I will take a bright new penny to pay for the egg, and tell her I am very very sorry. Then perhaps she will call back that horrid imp.'

So he washed his hands and face, brushed his hair, and took a bright new penny with him next door. Dame Bollo opened the door and asked him what he wanted.

'Please, Dame Bollo, I have come to confess a very naughty thing I did last week,' said the pixie. 'I took an egg when you were out, and now I have come to pay you a penny for it. The egg was a magic one, and a horrid imp came out of it, and has been living with me ever since. Would you please make him come back to you?'

'Well I never!' said Dame Bollo, surprised. 'I wondered what had happened to that egg, but I was very glad to see it gone, for *I* didn't want the nasty little imp! One of my hens, who used to belong to a witch, sometimes lays a magic egg like that, and I'm always careful not to let it hatch. Ho ho, what a joke! So you've got the imp, have you? Well, you can keep him!'

'Oh, Dame Bollo! I don't want him!' cried Pickle, in despair. 'He's perfectly horrid! He makes me work so hard, and you should just see my cottage now – it's like a new sixpence! And my garden too.'

'Well, and why shouldn't your cottage be neat and tidy?' asked Dame Bollo. 'It's always been a disgrace, as I've told you often enough. It seems to me it's a very good thing that imp's there, to see you do things properly!'

Poor Pickle began to cry.

'Well, I shan't go back home again if that horrid imp is to live with me,' he said. 'I shall pack my bag and go far away. I do think you are horrid not to tell me how to get rid of him, Dame Bollo.'

'And I think *you* are very horrid to have stolen an egg of mine,' said the old dame, crossly. 'It just serves you right!'

Pickle cried so many tears that he suddenly saw that he was standing in a puddle. Dame Bollo saw the puddle too, and felt sorry for the little pixie.

'Well,' she said, speaking in a kinder voice, 'well – perhaps I'll help you. All you've got to do is to say "Pigs and whistles" to that imp. Then he'll go.'

'Will he really?' cried Pickle. 'But why will he go when I say that?'

'Oh, *I* don't know!' said Dame Bollo. 'Why

does anyone do anything? But I warn you, Pickle, the Pixie – if ever I see that cottage of yours getting dirty and untidy again, I'll send you that imp to worry you, as sure as eggs are eggs!'

Pickle ran off to his cottage. He flung open the door, and looked round for the imp. There he was, sitting by the fire reading the paper, with his feet up on the mantelpiece.

'Shut the door, there's a draught,' said the imp, crossly.

Pickle left the door open, and walked over to the imp. He pointed his finger at him and spoke loudly.

'Pigs and whistles!' he said.

The imp leapt to his feet in fright. He turned a curious green colour, and became suddenly about half his size. Then, to Pickle's enormous surprise, he leapt straight up the chimney and disappeared.

'Ooh!' said Pickle, pleased. 'He's gone!'

The little pixie heaved a big sigh, picked up the dropped newspaper and sat down in his comfortable armchair to read it. It was the first time for a long while that he had been able to do that, and he *did* enjoy it!

Pickle has kept his cottage very spick and

span ever since; he is so afraid that that horrid imp might come back. Nobody knows where he went to, and nobody wants to know, either!

As Like As Two Peas
In A Pod

One day, Mollie was going through the wood wheeling Baby Jim in his pram, when she saw a little girl. She was most beautifully dressed, sitting under a tree, reading a book.

The little girl looked up when Mollie came near – and then she jumped to her feet in surprise, and Mollie, too, stared in astonishment – for the little girls were as alike as two peas in a pod!

They each had curling golden hair and blue eyes, straight little noses and a dimple in the chin. Really, you couldn't possibly tell one from the other.

'You *are* like me!' said Mollie.

'And you *are* like me!' said the rich little girl. 'Isn't it funny? Why, I don't believe our own mothers would know us from one another if we were dressed alike! I feel just as if I were looking in a mirror when I look at you!'

Mollie sat down by the rich little girl and they began to talk.

'My name's Rosemary,' said the little girl, 'and I live in that great big house on the hill. You can see it from here.'

'My name's Mollie,' said Mollie, 'and I live in that tiny cottage you can see through the trees.'

'I'm an only child,' said Rosemary, with a sigh. 'I have a very dull time.'

'I've six brothers and sisters, besides Baby Jim,' said Mollie. 'Oh, I wish I were you, Rosemary! It must be lovely to be the only one, and never have to wear dresses that have been worn by older sisters, and never be teased by brothers, and never have to take Baby out when you want to play! And have lovely cakes every tea-time, and—'

'Oh, Mollie, and I wish I were *you!*' said Rosemary. 'Goodness me, you've no idea how dull it is not to have any brothers or sisters to play with, not even a darling baby. I'd change places with you any day!'

The two little girls stared at one another,

and the same idea came into each golden
head.

'Let's change places just for a week!' they
cried both together.

'What fun!' shouted Mollie. 'I shall have all
your toys to myself, with nobody to snatch
them away!'

'What fun!' cried Rosemary. 'I shall have
heaps of brothers and sisters to play with!'

It didn't take more than five minutes for the
two children to change clothes. When Mollie
was dressed in Rosemary's, she looked for all
the world like the rich little girl, and as for
Rosemary, she looked exactly like Mollie.

'Take Baby Jim for a walk through the
wood,' said Mollie, 'and then go back to my
cottage to help my Mother to lay the dinner.
I hope you get on all right.'

'You must walk back to the big iron gates,'
said Rosemary, 'and you'll be just in time for
dinner. I've a nurse and a governess, and
they're both very strict, so I hope you won't
get into any trouble.'

'What about your Mother?' asked Mollie.
'Is she nice? Mine's lovely.'

'So is mine,' said Rosemary, 'but she is
always out at parties and dances, so I don't

see nearly enough of her. Still, she may perhaps come and kiss you goodnight.'

The two little girls said goodbye, promising to meet again in the same place the following week. Then Rosemary went happily towards the tiny cottage, wheeling Baby Jim and talking to him, whilst Mollie made her way towards the big iron gates, her heart beating in excitement to think of all the lovely things she would be able to do.

Just as she got there, she heard a gong

booming out, and a nurse dressed all in white came hurrying up.

'Miss Rosemary!' she cried to Mollie. 'Wherever have you been? You are late, you naughty girl. Come along and wash your hands at once.'

'But they're quite clean,' said Mollie.

'That doesn't matter,' said the nurse, crossly. 'You know you have to wash before every meal.'

She took Mollie to a most beautiful bathroom and washed her hands in hot water. Then she brushed Mollie's hair very hard indeed, tied a fresh ribbon on it, and took her into a very wonderful nursery.

Mollie looked round in delight. The paper on the walls was full of nursery rhyme pictures. The furniture was all white, with ducks, lambs and cats painted on it. On the table was a dinner service with Bo Peep and her sheep on every plate and dish. It was all most exciting.

'What's for dinner?' asked Mollie, sitting down hungrily. 'I hope it's duck and green peas, or something exciting like that – with ice-cream afterwards!

'It's only rude little girls that talk about their

dinner like that,' said the nurse. 'And good gracious me! Duck and green peas! Ice-cream! Whoever heard such nonsense? You know quite well that you are only allowed ice-cream as a very special treat.'

A maid came into the room, carrying a dish of boiled fish, which Mollie had always hated. The nurse put some on her plate, poured some white sauce over it, and gave her a boiled potato. Mollie looked at her dinner in dismay. Was this all that a rich little girl had? Why, at home they would be having roast beef, dumplings, and at least two kinds of vegetables!

She ate her fish gloomily, and thought it was horrid. But perhaps the pudding would be lovely!

But what a shock when it came! It was a little rice pudding and nothing else at all! Mollie could have cried.

'Can't I have some treacle with it?' she asked. 'I hate rice pudding by itself.'

'What a naughty, rude little girl you are today!' said the nurse. 'Fancy finding fault with a lovely rice pudding like that! I'm sure there are lots of poor little girls who would be very glad indeed to eat it.'

Mollie thought of her home. They would be

having ginger pudding today, because Mother had promised one for a treat. But she didn't say any more, for she was really rather afraid of the nurse.

She ate half her rice pudding, and left the rest on the plate. But the nurse made her finish it all up, and although she didn't want to, she had to.

'Now go and clean your teeth,' said the nurse. Then you must have your half-hour's rest before you do your afternoon's lessons.'

Mollie listened in horror. Lessons in the afternoon? Why, she only went to school in the mornings at home! And why should she have half an hour's rest? She wasn't a bit tired. And what a nuisance to have to clean her teeth! She did them twice a day at home, but she supposed she would have to do them after every meal now.

She cleaned her teeth, and then the nurse took off her dress and made her lie down on a lovely soft bed in a beautiful night nursery. Mollie waited till she had gone out of the room, and then she jumped up to look at all the lovely things. She longed to open the toy cupboard in the other nursery, and she peeped out of the door to see if anyone was there.

No, the room was empty! The little girl crept into the day nursery and ran to the toy cupboard. Oh, what lovely things were there! There were dozens of dolls, heaps of doll's clothes, a big Noah's ark, and on a little shelf by themselves, a great many books.

Mollie took out one of the dolls, and wished she could show it to Jeannie, her little sister. What fine games they could have with it! Then suddenly she heard a noise and the nursery door opened. It was the nurse!

'Miss Rosemary!' she cried, angrily. 'What a naughty girl you are today! What are you doing out of bed? You know quite well you mustn't get up till I come and fetch you. Go straight back. I shall tell your governess how naughty you've been, and ask her to punish you.'

Mollie crept back to the bed, her eyes full of tears. It seemed as if rich little girls couldn't do anything without being naughty! She did hope the governess wouldn't be very strict. Mollie wasn't *very* good at lessons, and she was afraid that she wouldn't know nearly enough to please the governess.

In a little while the nurse came to fetch her. She put a clean frock on Mollie, a perfectly

lovely one Mollie thought, washed her face and hands again, brushed her hair, and then took her into the day nursery, where the governess sat, all ready for lessons.

Oh dear, how strict she looked! She wore big glasses, and her hair was brushed tightly back from her face, which was thin and cross-looking. Mollie thought of the jolly, laughing teacher she had at the village school, and how she wished she were back there that afternoon, instead of in front of this clever-looking governess!

'I'm afraid Miss Rosemary has not been

very good since you left her this morning,' said the nurse. 'I must ask you to be very strict with her, Miss Brown, for she really has a very naughty mood on.'

Miss Brown frowned at Mollie and told her to sit down.

'I will hear your six times table first,' she said.

Now Mollie had only just reached six times at school, and hadn't learnt it really properly. So she began to stammer through it, making a dreadful number of mistakes. Miss Brown was not at all pleased.

'I thought I told you to learn it properly this morning,' she said. 'You will have to learn it this evening instead of riding on your pony.'

Poor Mollie! She did so want to ride on a pony, and now she wouldn't be able to. Miss Brown set her some writing to do next, and then some sums, both of which the little girl managed to do, though not very well. Then she had to read.

'You are not reading nearly so well as usual,' said Miss Brown. 'I don't think you are trying, Rosemary. Now, wake up, please! What is the matter with you today?'

It was dreadfully dull having lessons all by

herself. It was much more fun at school, where there were lots of other boys and girls. Still, perhaps playtime would come soon, and she could go out into the garden for ten minutes.

'Can't I go out to play yet?' Mollie asked at last.

'Go out to play?' said Miss Brown, in surprise. 'I don't know what you mean. You know quite well that you don't have any playtime in afternoon school.'

Mollie said no more. She wondered what Rosemary would be doing at her home. Perhaps helping Mother to iron, or picking some flowers to put on her table. Mollie wished she were there, too, instead of doing lessons all this lovely sunny afternoon.

At last they came to an end. Miss Brown packed up the books, told Mollie she might have five marks out of ten for her afternoon's work, which was very bad, and sent her away to wash her hands for tea.

Mollie wondered what there would be for tea.

'I expect there'll be three or four different sorts of jam,' she said, 'and heaps of cakes, and perhaps jelly in little glasses. Oh my, what a feast I shall have!'

But, goodness me! There was only brown bread and butter, a pot of honey, and one very plain cake without even a currant in it.

'Is that all there is for tea?' asked Mollie in dismay. The nurse looked up from her sewing.

'Well, really, Miss Rosemary!' she said. '*All* there is for tea! I should like to know what else you expect! And let me tell you this – Miss Brown says you have not done your lessons well, so you must go without cake today.'

Mollie sat down at the table with a frown . She helped herself to bread-and-butter and honey, thinking of the home-made jam that would be on the table at home, and the great big currant cake Mother would have baked today. There might be little chocolate buns, too if Mother had had time. And it would be so noisy and jolly with everybody there – not a bit like this, quiet and dull, with nobody to say a word to except the cross old nurse!

'Please can I go out on the pony?' she asked after tea, hoping that Miss Brown had forgotten to say anything to the nurse about her six times table.

'No, indeed!' said the nurse at once. 'Miss Brown said you must learn your six times table instead, as well you know. And let me tell you this, Miss Rosemary – it's very early to bed you'll go tonight if I have any more nonsense from you! Now sit down and learn your table at once, and don't say another word till you know it.'

Mollie sat down with her table book. She tried hard to learn her table, and at last she knew it. The nurse heard her say it and said yes, she knew it quite well at last.

'Now you may go out to play in the garden for a little while,' she said. So out ran Mollie, very glad indeed to be free for a little time. What glorious gardens they were! And, oh, the flowers! Mollie had never seen so many in all her life.

'I'll pick some to put in the middle of the nursery table,' she thought. 'They will look lovely there. And, oh, my goodness, just look at those strawberries!'

In a trice the little girl was having a glorious feast. She picked strawberry after strawberry, and then she gathered a lovely bunch of roses. But suddenly she heard an angry shout, and out came a gardener from a greenhouse.

'Miss Rosemary!' he cried. 'Oh, you naughty little girl! Whatever will your Mother say when she sees you've picked all those

roses? Why, they're meant for the dinner table tonight! And just look at your mouth! You haven't been picking the strawberries, have you? Didn't your Mother say you weren't to take any?'

The gardener took her by the hand and led her back to the nursery, where he told the nurse all that Mollie had done. She *was* angry!

'Well, you must go straight to bed!' she said. 'I really don't know what has happened to you today, Miss Rosemary. How *could* you pick all those flowers and eat those strawberries? You know very well you're not allowed to pick anything in the garden at all.'

Mollie thought of the little cottage garden at home, and the old rose trees that grew everywhere, and the apple trees and plum trees that any of the children might pick from, if they wished to. Then she looked at the clock to see if it really were anywhere near bedtime.

It was six o'clock! Mollie went to bed at half-past seven at home, with Jeannie and Tom, and they had a glorious time, pillow-fighting and romping. She couldn't, really couldn't, even for a punishment go to bed so early. Why, it was only Baby Jim's bedtime!

'I don't see why you should make me go to bed a whole hour and a half before my proper bedtime,' she said to the nurse. 'It would be quite enough punishment if I went at seven.'

'Don't be silly,' said the nurse, crossly. 'You know perfectly well that your ordinary bed-time is half-past six. I don't know what you mean by talking about going at *seven!*'

'Goodness!' thought Mollie in horror. 'Does Rosemary have to go to bed at half-past six every night? Why, she doesn't have any time for play at all! Lessons in the morning, lessons in the afternoon, and early to bed! Gracious me, it isn't any fun at all to be a rich little girl!

It's so lonely, too – there's nobody to laugh or joke with.'

The nurse put her to bed without saying another word, for she really was very much puzzled with the little girl. She didn't know that it wasn't Rosemary at all, but another child, and she couldn't think what had happened to make the little girl so naughty.

Soon Mollie was in bed, and she suddenly thought of her own mother, who always came to tuck her up and say goodnight. She wondered if Rosemary's mother would come and see her. If she couldn't have her own darling mother, well, it would be better than nothing if she could have someone else's mother to kiss her goodnight.

So she lay there and waited. And presently the door opened and a most beautiful lady came in. It was Rosemary's mother, and she was a little like Mollie's own mother to look at. But what a beautiful dress she had on! It was like a golden mist floating all round her. She had a diamond necklace on, and a lovely shining pin in her hair. Mollie thought she had never seen anyone so like a fairy in her life.

She held out her arms to the lovely lady,

longing to hug her. But the lady shook her head.

'Nurse says you've been naughty today,' she said sternly. 'I shan't kiss you good-night, Rosemary, when you're not good. Really, I don't know what should make you naughty. You have a very happy life with everything you want. If you were a poor little girl you would be very glad of all the lovely things here. Now go to sleep and wake up a better little girl in the morning.'

'Oh, please, do let me kiss you, even if you won't kiss me!' said Mollie, thinking that it would be a dreadful thing if she didn't get a goodnight kiss at all.

'No, Rosemary,' said the lovely lady. 'You'd only spoil my new frock. Now good-night and go to sleep.'

She went out of the room and Mollie lay quite still, thinking of her own mother, who always, always kissed her goodnight, no matter how naughty she had been, and who didn't mind at all if her dress was crumpled or crushed.

'I *have* been a silly girl,' thought Mollie, miserably. 'Oh, how ever can I go through a whole week like this? I simply can't! Oh,

Jeannie and Tom and Baby Jim, I do miss you! And Mother, I do want you too! I want my own bed even though it isn't soft like this one. I want my own nightie, even though it hasn't beautiful lace and ribbons like this one I'm wearing now. I want to be a poor little girl with lots of brothers and sisters, not a rich one without anyone to play with or love!'

Poor Mollie! The tears rolled down her cheeks, and she lay in the soft little bed hour after hour, thinking of her own home. Then at last, when a clock somewhere struck midnight, she could bear it no longer. She got up and dressed herself, stole downstairs, let herself out of a door, and ran home as fast as ever she could.

When she reached the cottage, she threw a stone up at her bedroom window. Soon Rosemary looked out, and was most astonished to see Mollie. She ran downstairs and went out to meet her.

'Why have you come back?' she asked. 'The week is only just begun!'

'I know!' said Mollie. 'But I couldn't bear it any longer. I want to come back to my own home and brothers and sisters and have my own Mother. Don't you want to go back to your lovely home, too?'

'No,' said Rosemary. 'I don't. Why, I've had the most glorious time today! I've never had so many people to play with in my life! And oh, my goodness, the lovely dinner and tea we had! Roast beef and dumplings and ginger pudding, and for tea there were *two* kinds of jam, a currant cake and chocolate buns! And no horrid strict Nurse to scold me for eating too much! Only your darling mother sitting with Baby Jim on her knee, smiling at us all!'

'Well, Rosemary, you can come and see me as often as you like, and play with us all,' said Mollie. 'But really and truly, you *must* let me come home again, and you must go back to *your* home, too. I was ever so miserable – why, your mother wouldn't even let me kiss her good-night in case I crumpled her lovely frock.'

'Well, I'll go back,' said Rosemary, with a sigh. 'But goodness me, Mollie, I can't think why you ever wanted to leave such a lovely home and family! I shall come and see you all again and often!'

It didn't take the two girls long to change over their clothes once more. Mollie slipped on her own nightie, and Rosemary dressed in her own clothes. Then they said goodbye. Rosemary ran off to her home, and Mollie slipped upstairs in delight to her own little bed.

And next day what a surprise her Mother got! No one was so happy or so helpful as Mollie! She couldn't do enough for her Mother, and she sang like a lark as she went about the little jobs it was her duty to do. Who wanted to be a rich little girl, and live in a great big beautiful house all alone? Not Mollie! She was happy enough now to be one of eight, teased and played with all day long!

Rosemary often came to see her, and soon

became the children's best playmate. Mollie's Mother was astonished to see a little girl so like her own.

'Why!' she said one day, 'I do believe if you two changed clothes with one another, I shouldn't know I'd got Rosemary instead of Mollie!'

Mollie and Rosemary smiled at one another when they heard that – but they didn't tell why!

The Midnight Elves

There was once a poor tailor who had hardly any work to do. He had a wife and four little children, and though he was willing to work all day long, he could not get enough work to fill even two hours. His children went hungry, and his poor wife wept to see them asking for bread.

One night the tailor went to bed more unhappy than ever before. He had had no work at all that day, and could not give his wife even a penny to buy bread. He tossed and turned in his hard bed, and did not get a wink of sleep.

He heard the clock strike twelve, and after that he heard something else. It sounded like a scraping and scratching at the window-pane.

'Whatever can it be?' wondered the tailor. 'Is it a cat trying to get in?'

The scraping and scratching went on. Soon the tailor got up and opened the window. Outside stood a company of tiny elves, all dressed in bright green. The moon shone down on them, and lit up their tiny faces.

'Are you Snips the Tailor?' asked the foremost one.

'Yes,' said Snips, greatly wondering.

'Have you still got that roll of blue cloth you had yesterday?' asked the elf, eagerly. 'I saw it when I peeped into your window.'

'Yes,' said Snips, again. 'Why do you ask?'

'We are in a great fix,' said the elf, 'and we wondered if you would help us. Our master, the Prince of Dreamland, is holding a ball at dawn today, and has commanded us to appear before him at cock-crow wearing blue suits to match his new carriage. Alas! We have made a mistake, as you see, and are all in green! We dare not appear before the prince like this, and not knowing what else to do, we have come to you!'

'You want me to make suits for all of you before dawn?' said the tailor in amazement. 'But I have never made clothes for such little folks before – I should not know how to!'

'Yes, you would,' answered the elf. 'We have often seen you making clothes for your children's dolls. We are much the same size. Oh, we beg of you, grant us our wish, and you will never regret it.'

The little creature spoke so earnestly that the tailor could not help granting his request. He bade them come in, and then he led the way to his work-room. He took down the roll of fine blue cloth, and began to cut it into strips. There were ten of the little folk, and the tailor reckoned he had just enough stuff. He was sad to cut up his beautiful cloth, for it was the only thing he had left to sell.

As he was busy fitting the cloth to the tiny elves his wife came gliding into the room. She had missed him from their bed, and had come to seek him. She stared in astonishment to see the little company of elves standing on the work-table.

Her husband told her what had happened, and she listened in surprise.

'I will sew on the buttons and make the button-holes,' she said, 'then the suits will certainly be ready in time.'

All night long the tailor and his wife worked
hard. Fifteen minutes before cock-crow ten
little blue suits lay ready on the table.

The elves quickly put them on, did up all
the buttons, and shouted in joy to see how
nicely the suits fitted them.

'Thank you a thousand times!' they cried,
and off they flew to attend their master, the
Prince of Dreamland. The tailor and his wife
were very tired, and putting their heads down
upon the table, they slept.

When the sun was up, and all the children

were awake and crying for something to eat, they awoke. They looked round the work-room, and remembered how they had spent their night. Snips arose, and taking up the few pieces of blue cloth still left, he went to put them away in the cupboard.

But what a surprise when he opened the door! Inside the cupboard were bales upon bales of magnificent cloth. There was cloth of silver and cloth of gold. There was a bale of rainbow-hued silk, such as the tailor had never seen in his life before! There was also a pile of rich cloth all embroidered with flashing gems.

'Look!' cried Snips, in amazement. 'Where did this come from?'

'From the elves!' said his wife in delight. 'This is their return for your kindness to them last night! Oh, Snips, put some of this stuff in the window! You will soon have all the work you want, for there is not another tailor in the kingdom who has such beautiful cloths as these!'

So Snips put the cloth in the window, and soon customers came pouring in. Never had they seen such beautiful stuffs before, and everyone wanted a dress made of this, or a coat made of that.

Then who should come by in his carriage, but the King of that country himself! When he saw the tailor's window, he stopped in surprise. His eye caught sight of the gem-studded cloth, and he jumped out of the carriage eagerly.

'Ho, tailor!' he said. 'You shall make me my new cloak of that stuff in your window! Here is a purse of gold in payment for the cloth. You shall have another when the cloak is finished.'

How excited the tailor and his family were! How Snips worked and worked! But no matter how much of his lovely new cloths he used, the cupboard was always full.

One day Snips was so rich that he left his tiny cottage and went to a fine house in the middle of the town. He took with him the old cupboard, and folks laughed at him.

'What does he want with that old thing?' they said to one another. 'He might well have left that behind!'

But Snips knew better. He was not going to leave his good luck behind him. Never again did he hear of the ten little elves, though for many years he kept the little green suits they

had left behind in case they returned again for them.

But they never did – so now his grandchildren use them for their dolls. They always have to put the little suits away very carefully after playing with them, for as Snips their grandfather says – 'You never know when the elves might ask for them back!'

Juggins, the Giant

Once upon a time, a good many years ago now, there lived a giant called Juggins. He was rather stupid, but very strong and savage, and wherever he settled down to live the people became frightened and ran away.

Juggins was proud of his great strength. He boasted of it all day long, and dear me, he certainly was strong! He once leaned against a house when he was tired, and down it went, clitter-clatter! Another time he stamped his foot in a rage and made a hole big enough to take a horse and cart! As for his voice, you could hear it a mile away, and people often thought a storm was coming when all the time it was simply Juggins shouting at his dog!

One day he came to live in the peaceful

village of Hideaway. Juggins had heard that the finest, fattest pigs were grown there, and as he was very fond of bacon he thought it would be a splendid idea to go to Hideaway, settle down there and frighten the people into giving him bacon every day for breakfast.

Everyone was horrified when Juggins strode into their peaceful village, his hob-nailed boots making a clatter like the noise of twelve wagons. They rushed to their doors and windows, and groaned when they saw Juggins.

'Now there will be no peace or happiness for anyone!' said High-hat, the head of the

111

village. 'This giant is a robber and a bully. We must put up with him as best we may.'

'Why should we put up with him?' cried Snippety, a small gnome in a red suit. 'Aren't you head of our village, High-hat, and supposed to be clever enough to look after us and save us from people like this giant Juggins?'

High-hat frowned. Snippety was always saying things like that. High-hat was lazy and didn't always do his duties well, and he was half afraid of the sharp little gnome, Snippety.

'Hold your tongue,' said High-hat to Snippety, frowning at him. 'I am about to call a meeting to decide what we shall do about Juggins.'

So the meeting was called – but nobody seemed to be able to think of anything that would send Juggins away. High-hat rubbed his long nose and brought out his plan.

'Let us offer Juggins fifty pounds of our best bacon to go away,' he said. 'He is so fond of bacon that he will probably accept that and go. What do you think friends?'

Everyone nodded his head and agreed, mournfully – everyone, that is, except Snippety, who at once jumped to his feet and shouted: 'No! No!'

'And why do you say "No! No!"?' asked High-hat, in a very cold voice.

'Because you are going to do the very thing that will make Juggins stay here longer than ever!' cried Snippety. 'As soon as he tastes fifty pounds of our best bacon he will say to himself: "Ha! Delicious! Best bacon I've ever tasted in my life! I shall stay here for ever and make the people give me my breakfast every day of the year." '

All the little folk nodded their heads. 'Quite right, quite right!' they said, more mournfully than ever.

'Well, since you are so clever, perhaps you will tell us how *you* would make the giant go?' said High-hat, in a very nasty sort of voice.

'Certainly, certainly!' said Snippety. 'Juggins is a strong and fierce giant, but he is very stupid. I think I could outwit him, if you will let me try!'

'Good for old Snippety!' cried everyone except High-hat. 'Good old Snips! Always got an idea haven't you, Snips?'

'Well, usually,' said Snippety, looking modest. 'It's better to wear a cap to keep your brains warm, than to do what some people do – wear a high hat to hide an empty head!'

High-hat nearly boiled over with rage, but everyone laughed so much that he couldn't make himself heard. He put on his high hat and stalked out of the room in disgust. Nobody minded him going at all. They all wanted to know what Snippety's plan was.

He told them. 'I shall challenge the giant to three feats of strength,' he said, 'and I shall beat him at every one of them! That will scare him so much that he will go and never come back again!'

'But, Snippety, the giant is MUCH stronger than you!' cried the gnomes. 'He will beat you at everything and then he will probably eat you for your impudence.'

'Leave it to me, leave it to me,' said Snippety grandly. 'All *you've* got to do is to come and see the three tests of strength and cheer me for all you're worth when I win them.'

'Oh, we'll do that all right!' cried all his friends, and after that the meeting broke up. Snippety went off to the hill where Juggins lived in a great cave, and called on him. The giant poked his head out of the cave, and even bold little Snippety felt a bit funny inside when he saw those great staring eyes and horrid big teeth.

'Good afternoon, Giant Juggins,' said Snippety, bowing politely. 'I am Snippety-Snappety-Snorum, the great and only strong man in the world. I may seem little to you, but my strength is marvellous. I can squeeze water from a stone, and kick lightning from a rock!'

The giant blinked his big eyes in astonishment that such a little manikin could boast so loudly.

'Pooh!' he said, 'you do not know what you say! I am Juggins, the strongest giant in the world. I could break you in half just by curling my little finger round you.'

'I dare say you could!' said Snippety, taking a step backwards, but not showing a bit of fear. 'Well, Juggins, what about seeing who is the stronger of us two, me or you?'

'What! now, do you mean?' asked Juggins, preparing to crawl out of his cave.

'No, no,' said Snippety, hastily. 'We must have people to judge between us and to say who wins. There must be a prize, too. If you win, you shall have a hundred fat pigs – and if I win I can have the treasure you have hidden in that cave of yours!'

Juggins grinned. It sounded easy to him, and his mouth watered at the thought of a hundred pigs for his own.

'Very well,' he said. 'What shall the tests be?'

'Can you kick dust from a hard rock?' asked Snippety. 'I can!'

'So can I!' said the giant, boastfully. 'I know I can kick more than you, so that shall be one test.'

'And can you squeeze water from cricket balls?' asked Snippety. 'I can!'

Juggins looked doubtful. 'Well,' he said,

'I've never had cricket balls big enough to try, but if *you* can, well *I* can, for certain sure!'

'Right,' said Snippety, 'that's test number two. Now for the last one. In our big pond there are two water-turtles, great big chaps. I can pull one out on the end of a rope, even though he tries his best to pull against me. Could you pull the other out, do you think?'

'Of course!' said Juggins, readily. 'You can go back and tell your friends that we will have these tests on Saturday, in the field near the pond. And, by the way, after I've beaten you I shall probably eat you. Have you thought of that?'

'Of course I haven't,' said Snippety, 'because, my dear fellow, you won't beat me! *Good* morning!'

The giant stared angrily after the cheeky gnome and made up his mind to punish him well when he got hold of him. But Snippety didn't seem to feel the giant's anger, and sauntered off gaily with his pointed cap well on one side.

He told his friends that Saturday was the day fixed for the three tests, and then he began to be very busy. He got out his tall boots and put them on the table in readiness. Then, curiously enough, he swept his chimney! He got a sack of soot from his chimney and looked pleased. Then he did a strange thing! He filled his boots almost up to the top with soot! He also took a pair of gloves and filled those with soot, too. He grinned to himself as he did this, and chuckled loudly.

Next he went to order two large cricket balls to be made for the giant to squeeze – but he did not order any small ones for himself. No, he simply took two oranges and painted them very carefully with bright red paint and then put them on his window-sill to dry. They looked exactly like cricket balls when they were finished! Snippety was delighted.

The next thing he did was to buy two long pieces of stout rope, and when Saturday morning came he went down to the pond, very early, before anyone else was up. He whistled softly, and a large water-turtle swam up to the surface.

'Hallo, Hardback!' said Snippety. 'Do me a favour, will you? Go and tie the end of this rope to that enormous old buried tree in the bottom of the pond – you know, the one that fell in twelve years ago when it was struck by lightning.'

The turtle took the rope and vanished. It came up again in two minutes and looked at Snippety with its small, bright eyes. It was fond of this cheeky gnome, who so often came to feed it.

'And now, Hardback,' said Snippety, 'just one more thing. You see this second rope, don't you? Well, tie it to the roots of a water-plant, and listen hard for me to shout this morning. I shall pull this rope, and shout all the time. Don't take any notice of my shouting till you hear me say: 'Now then, you miserable Hardback, come up with you!' Then you must make a great disturbance in the pond, untie the rope from the roots, and hang on to it yourself. I shall then pull you out of the water. But don't untie the rope that is tied to the old tree, whatever you do!'

The turtle nodded its wrinkled head and took the second rope. It tied it carefully to the roots of a big water-plant, and then popped its head out of the water to see what was going to happen.

At midday, when the sun was high, the giant Juggins came stalking down the hill. He looked very grand and very fierce, for he had on a feathered hat, a big cloak that flew out in the wind and a most enormous sword that glittered in the bright sunshine. Nobody felt brave when they saw him, not even Snippety – but he was plucky, and he went forward to greet the giant.

'Where are the hundred pigs?' asked Juggins, looking round. Now Snippety hadn't bothered about those, because he felt so certain of winning – but Juggins was angry to find that the prize was not there. So there was a great delay whilst a hundred fat pigs were rounded up and put into a ring of hurdles. They made a great squealing, and the giant looked at them with pleasure. What a lot of fat bacon!

'The first test is to see who can kick the most dust out of this big rock here,' said Snippety boldly. 'Have you brought your biggest boots, Giant Juggins?'

'Yes,' said the giant, and he took from his back a most enormous pair of high boots. He meant to do the thing well, and show everyone what a strong, fierce fellow he was. Ho, ho! How they would quail and shrink when they saw what he could do!

He put on his boots and went to stand on the great rock. Then he began to kick and stamp on it. My goodness me, what a noise, what a clatter, what a shower of rocky fragments and splinters!

But there was no dust at all. Sparks flew from beneath the giant's feet, and everyone fled out of reach of the bits of rock that flew up into the air. Smash, crash, clatter, smash, crash, clatter, went the giant's feet. He was enjoying himself hugely.

'Well,' he said at last, quite out of breath. 'Is that enough for you, good people? Have I shown you how to kick dust out of a rock?'

'That is hardly dust,' said Snippety, picking up a large piece of rock. 'Still, we will see if I can do any better. Yours was certainly a remarkable performance, Juggins!'

The small gnome slipped on his big, sooty boots, and put on his sooty gloves. Then he stepped on to the rock and began to kick and stamp. The soot flew up out of his boots and rose in a great black cloud!

'OooooooooooOOOH!' cried everyone in the very greatest astonishment. Even Juggins was amazed, and opened his mouth wide in surprise. He got it full of soot and began to choke and cough.

'What a dust! What a dust!' cried all the

watching folk. 'Ooh, Snippety, how marvellous you are! Look at all the dust you are kicking out of the rock!'

Snippety, quite hidden in a cloud of black soot, began to clap his gloved hands together. At once more soot flew out and the cloud round him was thicker and blacker than ever. He began to choke and cough too, but he wouldn't give up! No, he kicked and danced, stamped and shuffled on the rock till he hadn't an ounce of breath left. It was the others who stopped him.

'Stop, Snippety, stop!' they cried. 'You have won! Even Juggins says you have won! He did not kick dust as you do, he simply kicked the rock to pieces!'

So Snippety stopped and came down from the rock, smiling all over his very black and dirty face.

'I raised some dust, didn't I?' he said. 'I'll have to go and wash before we have the next test. I am really very dirty.

Off he went and made himself clean. Then he picked up the two enormous cricket balls and the two small, painted oranges and set off to the field again, where the giant waited with everyone else.

'Test number two!' shouted Snippety, grandly. 'Two cricket balls for you, Juggins, and two small ones for me, just the right size to fit our hands. Now then, stand over there opposite to me, and at the word "Go!" squeeze the balls as hard as you can!'

'One, two three, *go*!' shouted High-hat, when they were both ready. The giant squeezed his cricket balls and they became soft and flabby – but no water came from them. But to everyone's great amazement, juice came out of the two balls held by Snippety and dropped slowly to the ground!

'Look at Snippety!' cried the watching folk. 'See, he is squeezing yellow water out of the balls! Oh, how strong and clever he is! He has won the second test too!'

The giant squeezed his cricket balls harder than ever, but it was no use – not a drop came out of them, and no wonder, either! In a temper he flung them into the air and they dropped into the pond with a splash! Snippety, half afraid that the giant might ask to see his balls was only too glad to do the same – and splash they went into the pond, where they were eagerly gobbled up by the surprised water-turtle!

'Now for the last test,' said Snippety, dancing up to the two ropes, and giving the giant one of them. 'See who can pull his turtle out of the pond first!'

The giant took hold of his rope and strained hard at it, thinking to pull the water-turtle out with a rush – but his rope was fastened to the long-sunk tree in the middle of the deep pond, and it barely stirred when he pulled. It was covered with mud, and had sunk deeply down.

Snippety pulled hard too, and danced about

as he pulled, shouting: 'Come on, there! Hey, come on there! Wait till I get you out of the water!'

But nothing came. The water-turtle was listening for the right words, and all that happened was that Snippety's rope pulled hard at the roots of the water-plant, but nothing else. Then the giant pulled his rope again. How he pulled! His face wrinkled up, his tongue stuck out, his forehead became wet – but no matter how he tried he could *not* pull a water-turtle out of the water.

Snippety pulled on his rope again, and this time he shouted loudly: 'Now then, you miserable Hard-back, come up with you!'

At once the listening turtle undid the rope from the plant-root and hung on to it himself. Snippety pulled hard and up came the water-turtle out of the pond with the end of the rope in his mouth!

'Snippety's won, Snippety's won!' yelled everyone, dancing madly about in glee. 'He's stronger than Juggins, the Giant! He's a fine fellow, is Snippety! He's better than a giant, so he is!'

Juggins stood listening to this, a great frown on his hot forehead. He was astonished when he saw the water-turtle come up out of the pond. Why, it wasn't very big – and if that silly little Snippety could drag a little creature like that out of the pond, why, he could too!

He suddenly began to pull again. Snippety was alarmed, because he didn't want the giant to find out the trick he had played on him.

'You don't need to pull up your turtle,' he said at once. 'I've won, Juggins. Spare yourself.'

But the giant was furiously angry now, and he pulled like a hundred bulls. The buried tree in the pond shifted a little and gave way about two inches. The giant felt it giving and tugged again. The tree moved once more, and Snippety became very much alarmed.

'Stop, I tell you,' he cried to the giant. 'There is a fearful water-creature in that pond, and perhaps it has got hold of your rope. If you pull it out it will eat us all up, and you too.'

The giant stopped in fear – but soon his anger came upon him again and he tugged with all his strength. And then, with a fearful gurgling, sucking noise, that enormous old tree came up out of the pond! It had stiff, dripping branches that looked like hair, and

the noise it made was most terrifying. Every-one shrieked in horror and tore off as fast as their legs would carry them.

'The water-monster! The water-monster! It will eat us all up! OooooooooooOOOH!'

'Run! Run!' cried Snippety to the frightened giant, who really thought he had pulled up a great monster. 'It will eat you first. Run for your life!'

Juggins dropped the rope and tore off, taking a quarter of a mile in each stride. In no time at all he was a thousand miles away, vowing never, never, *never* to return to the village of Hideaway, with its awful Snippety and its terrible water-monster!

As soon as he was gone, Snippety sat down and laughed till he cried. Then he called back the little folk and showed them that the monster was only the buried tree.

'We will dry it and cut it up for logs,' he said. 'Well, friends, am I not a smart gnome?'

'You are marvellous!' cried everyone, even High-hat. 'You shall have all the giant's treasure from his cave and we will make you head of the village, Snippety. And now, do *do* tell us how you squeezed juice from the cricket balls and how you kicked such black dust from the rock.'

But Snippety looked very wise and shook his head. 'No,' he said. 'Those are my secrets. I shall never tell you.'

And he never did tell anyone but the old water-turtle. The turtle told the frogs, and the frogs croaked the whole story out to one another in the Springtime. So now everyone knows, even you!

Fee-Fie-Fo the Goblin

Nobody knew where Fee-Fie-Fo came from, for he suddenly appeared one dark night with a barrow on which were all his belongings, and went to live in Twisty Cottage in the middle of Ten O'clock Village.

The other little folk were quite ready to make friends with him – but they soon found that Fee-Fie-Fo was a bad friend and a worse enemy! He was mean and stingy, cruel and dishonest, and he knew such a lot of magic that soon the folk of Ten O'clock Village were very much afraid of him.

'Can't we get rid of him?' they asked one another. But nobody could think of a way, and the months went on with the ugly little goblin living in the middle of the village, frightening the children, shouting at the dogs, and sending all the older folk hurrying home when he began to mutter spells that brought the thunder, or great gales that blew away their chimneys.

At last the folk of Ten O'clock sent to the pixie Tiptap who lived in a cave on the nearby hill. He was supposed to be very wise and very good. The little folk told him their trouble and he promised to do what he could for them. 'I will think it over,' he said, 'and I will send you my plan when I have finished it.'

So Ten O'clock Village waited in patience. At last the plan came, and the head man of the village called a meeting and read out the letter.

DEAR FRIENDS [it began],

Here is my plan. Prepare a birthday party for the great Wizard Hollabolla-boo. Say it is for his hundredth birthday and have a cake made with ninety-nine little candles on it and one bigger one in the middle. Invite Fee-Fie-Fo to the party. That is all. Leave the rest to me.

TIPTAP

So the little folk obeyed, and sent out invitations for Hollabolla-boo's hundredth birthday, though they had no idea at all who the great wizard was, and, indeed, had never even heard of him before!

One of the invitations went to Fee-Fie-Fo, and he wondered who in the world Hollabollaboo was. He must really go and see! He would show the hundred-year-old wizard that he, Fee-Fie-Fo, knew even more magic than a wizard! Ho, ho!

A big birthday cake was made by Dame Biscuit, the baker's wife, and Mister Tallow, the candle-man, put eleven rows of nine differently coloured candles on the cake, with a bigger blue candle in the middle.

The great day came. All the folk of the village went to the little hall where they had their meetings and their parties. There was an enormous table there, and in the middle was the cake. Around it were other plates of cakes and buns, and big mugs of milk.

Would Hollabolla-boo be there? Yes – he was! He sat at the head of the table, a small figure dressed in a flowing black cloak and pointed hat, with a long white beard. The little

131

folk bowed to him and took their places. Last of all Fee-Fie-Fo came stalking in.

'Ho, so you're Hollabolla-boo!' he said rudely to the wizard. 'I suppose you think because you are a hundred years old that you are the cleverest person in the world – but you don't know me – Fee-Fie-Fo, the mighty goblin! I can do more magic than anyone in the kingdom.'

'Sit down, Fee-Fie-Fo,' said the wizard in a stern voice. 'This is a party, not a fight. After tea, if you wish, we will see who is the cleverer, you or I!'

'Ha, I'll show you all a few things!' said Fee-Fie-Fo, glaring round in such a terrible way that everyone trembled and shook. He sat down and began his tea, muttering to himself and sticking his sharp elbows into the frightened gnomes next to him.

Nobody took any notice of Fee-Fie-Fo and soon he began to feel angry. His hair stood up straight on his head and sparks flew out of his eyes. He suddenly banged on the table and said: 'Cakes, come to me!'

He opened his mouth, and to the little folks' surprise and anger every single cake on the table flew into his wide mouth.

'What do you think of *that*?' said Fee-Fie-Fo, pleased to see everyone's amazement. 'Now look at this!'

He suddenly turned into a big brown bear and everyone scattered in fright – all except the wizard, who sat still at the table watching him. The goblin changed back to himself again, grinning. He clapped his hands and a fire sprang up from the floor, with green and blue flames that whistled like the wind. It was very strange to see.

'Well, Wizard!' said Fee-Fie-Fo, rudely, 'do you think you can better me in magic? I can change myself into anything in the world – a chair' – he changed into a chair in a trice, and then back again; 'a cat' – he turned into a black cat with white whiskers, and then back again; 'or even a thunderstorm!' At once he disappeared and a fearful thunderstorm raged for a few minutes round the little hall. Everyone screamed.

When the goblin was back again, the wizard spoke, very slowly and mockingly.

'You do no more than a twenty-year-old wizard can do,' he said to the surprised goblin. 'You can change into many things, but you cannot remain anything for more than one minute at a time.'

'That is not true!' cried the goblin at once. 'Tell me anything in the world to change into and I will do so and remain that thing for twenty minutes!'

'And suppose you become yourself again before the twenty minutes is up?' asked the wizard.

'Then I will go away and never come back, for I should be ashamed,' said the goblin, laughing.

'Then change into that middle candle that is on the birthday cake,' said the wizard.

'Easy!' cried the goblin and disappeared. The middle candle shook a little and a voice came from it. 'I will be in this candle for twenty minutes. Time me by the clock.'

The wizard took out a matchbox and struck a match. 'There is no need to time you by a clock,' he said. 'This candle will burn for twenty minutes, goblin.' He lighted the candle and everyone solemnly watched it burning.

It slowly grew smaller as it burned away. The goblin kept calling out rude things – but suddenly a strange fear fell on him. Suppose he burnt entirely away? If he did, he would not be able to go back to his goblin shape, for he would be gone with the candle.

'I am coming back!' he cried, when the candle had nearly burnt away.

'No, for the twenty minutes is not gone,' cried everyone. 'Oho, goblin, you are not so clever as you thought you were!'

'Well, I will NOT be burnt right away!' said the goblin's voice, and the candle shook on the cake. 'I am too clever for that!'

The candle fell over and the goblin suddenly appeared again. The wizard pointed at him. 'You could not do what you said you could,'

he said slowly. 'You must keep your word and go right away!'

'It's a trick, a trick!' shouted the goblin, in a rage.

'Ah, the wizard is cleverer than you!' shouted everyone in delight. 'He has tricked you. Go away, goblin, before he tricks you again!'

The goblin gave a mournful howl, leapt up the big chimney and disappeared. That was the end of him. The wizard dragged off his long beard, threw off his cloak and danced a merry jig round the room.

'It's Tiptap the pixie!' cried all the little folk and cheered him till they were hoarse. Then they all went out to get some more cakes, and had a really splendid party.

As for Fee-Fie-Fo, it is said he sometimes howls in the wind. When you hear him you must think of how easily Tiptap tricked him at that party long ago!

The Invisible Boy

There was once upon a time a boy who was really most inquisitive. He would poke his nose into everything, he asked thousands of questions each day, and his sharp little eyes never missed a single thing that happened.

That was how he came to see the little old wizard on the hillside. The wizard was hiding in the bracken, for he had heard Timmy's whistling, and he didn't want to be seen. But in his hat was a long blue feather, and this stuck up just a little way above the bracken.

Timmy's sharp, inquisitive eyes saw it. He stopped. What a strange thing! What was a long blue feather doing sticking out of the bracken like that? What bird could it be that was hiding there?

Timmy took two quick steps into the bracken and flung himself on the place where the feather was, meaning to catch and look at the bird he thought was hiding there. And to his enormous astonishment he found that he had got hold of a little old wizard!

He knew he must be a wizard because he wore the sort of cloak you see wizards wearing in pictures – a long red one with stars and moons shining all over it. Timmy was a little bit frightened, but very curious. He didn't let go but held on tightly to the startled wizard.

'What are you hiding for?' asked Timmy. 'I thought you were a bird.'

'Let go of my arm,' said the wizard. 'I've got to get home quickly.'

'Take me with you,' said Timmy, excitedly, very curious to see where the wizard lived.

'No,' said the wizard.

'Yes,' said Timmy.

'*No*,' said the wizard.

'YES!' shouted Timmy in such a fierce voice that the wizard trembled. He was very old and rather timid, so he said no more but led the way up the hillside. He came to a gorse-bush and crept underneath it. Timmy followed, scratching himself on the thorns, but much too excited to mind.

The gorse-bush leaned against the rocky hillside, and when Timmy had crawled under the bush he saw a big rock at the back. It had a yellow spot painted on it in the middle and when the wizard pressed this the rock opened like a door. He went inside the hill and Timmy followed, red with excitement. What an adventure!

Inside the hill was a large room which had a big fire at one end, with strange blue flames instead of red ones. A round table stood in the middle, turning round and round on one leg, humming a tune as it did so. There was a clock on the mantelpiece which had a proper face with eyes, nose and mouth, and every time it ticked it moved its eyes to and fro. Timmy thought it was very peculiar.

The wizard spoke sharply to the humming table. 'Be quiet! Can't you see I have a visitor?'

The table stopped its humming and came to a standstill. The clock on the mantelpiece made a rude face at Timmy, who at once made a rude face back. Then to his surprise the clock shot out a tiny fist and tapped him hard on the nose!

'Serves you right,' said the wizard to Timmy. 'You shouldn't make faces. You'd better be careful what you do here. You never know what might happen next.'

It was true. Even as Timmy looked round he saw the coal-scuttle walk to the fire, tip itself up and empty some coals on to the blue flames. Then it walked back to its place.

'How does it do that?' asked Timmy in astonishment. 'And oh my! Look at that chair! It's doing a sort of dance on the floor – and the table's started humming again!'

'*Will* you be quiet when you're told?' the

141

wizard said sharply to the table. It stopped humming again and the chair became still.

Timmy caught sight of a shelf on which were many bottles with all kinds of labels. He went to look at them.

'Don't poke your nose into my business,' said the wizard gruffly. 'Come away from those bottles. They have magic spells in them.'

But Timmy *had* to look at them. There was a blue bottle labelled: *If you drink this you will grow as big as a giant*. There was a green bottle labelled: *Drink this and grow small*. Then Timmy spied a tiny bottle with yellow liquid in and the label said: *Drink me and you will have donkey's ears*. Timmy didn't think he would like to try *that*!

Goodness, what strange bottles those were! The next one Timmy saw had a curious spotted liquid in it and the label said: *I will make you invisible*.

'Did you hear me say come away from those bottles?' said the wizard impatiently. 'You are just about the most inquisitive boy I've ever seen! I feel very annoyed with you, coming here like this, grabbing my arm all the way.'

'Oh, don't be annoyed,' said Timmy. 'Tell me how you make your magic? What do you

use? How do you know what to do? Do
you live all alone? Do you know any witches?'

'Don't ask so many questions,' said the
wizard. 'It's time for you to go now. If you
don't I'll turn you into an earwig and you
won't like that.'

Timmy paid no attention, though he might
have seen that the little wizard was getting
angry. He just went on asking him questions,
and if there is anything a wizard or a witch
hates most in the world it is being asked
questions!

'What is your name?' asked Timmy. 'How
old are you? Have you ever seen the Queen of
Fairyland? Have you a black cat like witches
have? Could you do some magic to show me?
Why do you wear a cloak like that? Why don't
you like your table to hum? Have you lived for
a long time? Have you . . .'

'BE QUIET!' yelled the wizard, clapping
his hands over his ears. 'I'll punish you if you
don't hold your tongue and get away from
here whilst there's time. I am getting VERY
ANGRY!'

'What do you do when you're angry?' asked
Timmy curiously. 'Do you go up in blue

smoke? Or do you just stamp about? Or do you . . .'

'I'll show you what I do when I'm angry,' said the wizard in a very quiet cold voice, staring hard at Timmy as he spoke. 'I change people into strange things. I wonder what you'd like to be? A mouse? A frog? An earwig? Perhaps you'd like to be a nice fat little pig? Yes, I'll turn you into a pig. You'll find lots of acorns on the hillside to eat. Now watch me, since you're so curious about everything. See . . . I take this yellow powder . . . and this blue feather . . . and this green water . . . and this pink lemon whose juice I squeeze over everything . . . then I stir the mixture with the wrong end of the feather, like this . . . and when I have stirred it thirty times you will have changed into a nice grunting little . . . pig!'

Timmy began to feel frightened. He watched the wizard stirring and stirring, and he tried to call out to stop him. But all he could say was a funny grunting noise!

'Oh!' he thought, 'I'm changing already! How dreadful! I must escape whilst there's time!'

But do you know, the door had vanished!

Yes, it was no longer there! There was nothing around Timmy but walls. It was dreadful. The wizard was stirring and counting as he stirred. He had got to twenty-one! Whatever was Timmy to do? He couldn't bear the thought of turning into a little pig, however nice and fat he would be.

He looked round him in despair – and then he suddenly caught sight of the strange bottles up on the shelf! And he saw the one with the spotted liquid in it. The label on it said: *I will make you invisible*. Timmy had read it only a few minutes back.

'Twenty-four, twenty-five,' counted the wizard, stirring hard. 'Twenty-six, twenty-seven, twenty-eight, twenty-nine . . .'

There wasn't a moment to waste. Timmy snatched up the bottle of spotted liquid, took out the cork and drank the bottleful. Ooh, it wasn't very nice! It tasted of cough medicine and burnt toast.

'Thirty!' said the wizard, loudly and stopped stirring. He looked round to see if Timmy had changed into a nice fat little pig – but Timmy wasn't there! No, the magic water had made him invisible so that no one could see him at all! He was there all right, but the wizard couldn't see him!

He had only just drunk the spotted water in time – another moment and he would have been a little pig. Now he was still a boy but he couldn't be seen.

The wizard was startled. He hadn't seen Timmy drink the Invisible Water. He couldn't think where he had gone to. He began to hunt for him. He looked under the table and behind the couch. He looked behind the curtain that hung at one end of the room. No Timmy anywhere.

'He must somehow have found the door

and gone,' said the wizard in great surprise. 'I wonder how he did that, because I bewitched the door away! Well, I'll put it back and see if that wretched inquisitive boy is anywhere on the hillside. Perhaps he changed into a pig after all!'

He chanted three strange words and the door appeared again in the wall. The wizard opened it and went out. Timmy went too, though the wizard didn't see him! The little old man looked everywhere but he could see no Timmy.

'Strange,' he said, 'very strange. I wonder where he is?'

'*HERE!*' yelled Timmy, right in his ear. The wizard was so startled that he fell straight into a gorse bush and sat there hardly daring to move. It was dreadful to hear a voice shouting in his ear and not see the person who was talking!

Timmy decided to go away quickly. He didn't know whether or not the wizard knew a spell to make him visible again. So off he went. Nobody could see him. Soon he began to whistle loudly.

He came near a cottage, where a woman was weeding her garden. She heard him

whistling and looked up. There was nobody there! How very strange!

'Good afternoon!' said Timmy and went on, chuckling to see the startled woman run indoors like a frightened hen.

'This is funny!' said Timmy. 'I'm going to enjoy myself!'

He soon came to his own street, and saw four of his friends playing marbles. Timmy went up and watched. He saw one boy cheat, and Timmy gave him a hard pinch.

'Ow! said the boy and looked round in surprise. 'Who pinched me? I'll fight him if he pinches me again!'

Timmy pinched him again, and the boy

stared round in astonishment. There was no one there.

'You're a cheat!' said Timmy.

'Who called me a cheat?' said the boy, fiercely looking round at the others.

'I did!' said Timmy and he took off the boy's cap and flung it to the ground. The boy was pale with fright, and he pushed his bag of marbles into the hands of the other astonished boys, saying: 'Yes, yes, I did cheat! I'm sorry! I won't do it again. Here, take my marbles and forgive me!'

'See that you never cheat again!' said Timmy, in a stern voice and walked off, whistling. The other boys stared after the invisible whistler in amazement. They couldn't make it out.

'It sounded like Timmy's voice!' said one. 'What a funny thing! We must have been dreaming!'

Timmy walked on past his own home. His mother was talking to her neighbour over a wall. She was a pretty little woman with a kind face. Timmy loved her very much. He went softly into the garden, picked a red rose and slipped it into his mother's hand. Then he kissed her softly on the neck and ran off.

'Oh, goodness me, who was that!' cried his mother, astonished. 'Did you see anyone come in, Mrs. Brown? Look, there's a lovely rose in my hand and someone kissed me on the neck? Now who could it be? I didn't see my boy Timmy about, did you?'

'No, I didn't,' said her neighbour in surprise. 'That rose suddenly appeared. Well, you're lucky, Mrs. Smith, to have roses coming out of the air like that!'

Timmy was pleased at his mother's surprise. It was fun being invisible. He went down the road and round the corner towards Long Hill. Halfway up was a heavy cart loaded with timber. One big horse was pulling it. The carter was a bad-tempered man known by all the boys around.

Timmy watched him. He took up his whip and slashed the horse. The poor beast strained to get quickly up the hill, but he was not quick enough for the carter. Slash! went the whip again.

'You stop that!' shouted Timmy, in a rage. 'Hey, stop that, I say, or I'll give you a good whipping myself!'

The carter looked round to see who had

spoken. He could see nobody at all. He slashed the horse again out of temper.

Then to his great surprise he felt the whip being taken from his hand and he saw it standing on the pavement. He got down to get it, thinking that he must be dreaming – and then the whip lifted itself up in the air and coiled neatly and sharply round the cruel carter's legs!

'Ow, ow!' he yelled in pain. 'Stop it! What's happening? Stop it! I'm hurt!'

'Well, you're getting no more than your horse,' said Timmy, in his ear. The carter jumped back in fright and once more looked all round the road. He couldn't see a soul anywhere! Slash! Crack! went the whip again and the carter howled loudly and jumped hastily up to his seat on the cart. The horse pulled his heavy load to the top of the hill, and Timmy watched him go, still holding the big whip in his hand.

'I won't ill-treat the horse again!' he heard the carter say again and again, for the man was afraid that the whip would come after him. Timmy laughed and went to the village pond. He threw the big whip right into the middle of it, and it sank down.

A bus came down the hill to the stopping-place at the bottom. Quite a crowd of people were there, waiting for it. There was an old lady, a woman with a baby, two children, a lame man, a woman carrying a big bag and a stout man with an umbrella. Timmy watched them. He saw the stout man elbowing everyone away so that he might get on first. He pushed away the children, he shoved a sharp elbow into the lame man's ribs, and he pushed right in front of the woman with the baby. Timmy ran down the hill and slipped into the bus with the crowd, not seen by any of them.

The stout man had taken a seat for himself, but the two children and the woman with the shopping bag had to stand. Timmy made up his mind to punish the man. When the bus stopped again and people began to get in, Timmy took off the man's hat and put it quickly on the floor, where it was at once trampled on.

'Oh, oh my new hat!' cried the man and he got up in a hurry to find his hat. At once his seat was taken by the woman carrying the heavy bag, and when he stood up with his crumpled hat there was no seat for him! Then

Timmy began to push against him and dig his elbows into his ribs, just as he had seen the man do to other people when trying to get on the bus. The man couldn't understand it. As soon as he looked round to see who had punched him in the back somebody seemed to hit him in the front, and yet he could never see who was doing it.

When the man took out his purse to pay his fare Timmy jerked it out of his hand, and some of the money fell into the shopping bag of the poor woman who was sitting nearby. She didn't see the coins fall into her bag — only Timmy saw, and he wasn't going to say anything about them! No, they would be a nice surprise for the poor woman, and it would serve the stout man right to lose a few shillings!

The stout man didn't like the bus at all. He couldn't understand all the strange things that kept happening. He made up his mind to get out at the very next stop, and out he got. So did Timmy. He dug his elbow into the man for the last time, and hissed: 'Don't shove and push next time you get on a bus!'

The man turned very pale and hurried off clutching his umbrella and his hat as if he thought someone was going to take them from him. Timmy laughed and strolled back the way the bus had come. What fun it was to be invisible!

But dear me, if Timmy had only known it, the magic was wearing off! Little bits of him were to be seen here and there – a button on his coat, a lace in one of his shoes, and the stud in his collar. A dog passing by saw the shoe lace going along by itself, and snapped at it. Timmy was surprised. He didn't know that any of him was showing.

'Go home!' he said to the dog, and the little creature, frightened by a voice that didn't seem to have an owner, turned and fled for his life!

Then Timmy's cricket belt became visible and could quite easily be seen. People stared in alarm as it came slowly through the air towards them. They couldn't see Timmy, and they were frightened to see a nice cricket belt travelling through the air by itself.

Then Timmy's face could be seen, but no body, and that frightened people more than ever! Even the big policeman at the corner turned a little pale when he saw a cricket belt,

a shoe lace, a collar-stud and a smiling face walking along all by themselves.

'I must have eaten something that disagreed with me,' said the policeman to himself. 'Dear me, to think that my nice dinner of sausage and potato should make my eyes go all funny and see things like that!'

Timmy met some of his friends. They stopped in alarm and pointed to Timmy's cheery face.

'Look! There's Timmy! But where's the rest of him? Hey, Timmy, what have you done

155

with the rest of your body? Have you left it at home?'

'No, it's here all right but you can't see it yet,' said Timmy. 'I've been to see a wizard and I drank some magic water and made myself invisible. I've had such fun! But my goodness me, I nearly got turned into a nice, fat little pig because I asked the wizard so many questions!'

'You always were inquisitive, Timmy,' said one of his friends. 'I told you that if you poked your nose into things you'd have a shock one day!'

'Well, I've certainly had a shock!' said Timmy, 'but I've had a great time too! Anyway, it's cured me of being inquisitive. I might not get off so easily next time! I shouldn't have liked to be invisible all my life long!'

'You're getting a neck now!' cried the boys in excitement. 'And there's one leg! Ooh, isn't it funny! Tell us all about your adventures, Timmy.'

So Timmy told all about the wizard on the hillside, and as he spoke he gradually became whole again – the other leg appeared, then his arms and hands and then his body. One knee took a long time to come, but after that he was invisible no longer.

'Oh Timmy, take us up the hillside and let's see the wizard!' begged the other boys. 'We shan't believe your story if you don't!'

So the next day Timmy took his friends up on the hillside. They crawled under the gorse-bush and pressed the yellow spot in the middle of the rock. It swung open like a door and the boys looked inside.

But all they could see was a rabbit-hole with a rabbit's woffly nose peeping round the corner. The rabbit looked at them with a surprised eye and fled.

'It might have been the wizard who had turned himself quickly into a rabbit!' cried the boys.

It *might* have been. I wonder if it was!

Join the RED FOX Reader's Club

The Red Fox Reader's Club is for readers of all ages. All you have to do is ask your local bookseller or librarian for a Red Fox Reader's Club card. As an official Red Fox Reader you only have to borrow or buy eight Red Fox books in order to qualify for your own Red Fox Reader's Clubpack – full of exciting surprises! If you have any difficulty obtaining a Red Fox Reader's Club card please write to: Random House Children's Books Marketing Department, 20 Vauxhall Bridge Road, London SW1V 2SA.

Other great reads from **Red Fox**

Further Red Fox titles that you might enjoy reading are listed on the following pages. They are available in bookshops or they can be ordered directly from us.

If you would like to order books, please send this form and the money due to:

ARROW BOOKS, BOOKSERVICE BY POST, PO BOX 29, DOUGLAS, ISLE OF MAN, BRITISH ISLES. Please enclose a cheque or postal order made out to Arrow Books Ltd for the amount due, plus 75p per book for postage and packing to a maximum of £7.50, both for orders within the UK. For customers outside the UK, please allow £1.00 per book.

NAME_____

ADDRESS_____

_____

Please print clearly.

Whilst every effort is made to keep prices low, it is sometimes necessary to increase cover prices at short notice. If you are ordering books by post, to save delay it is advisable to phone to confirm the correct price. The number to ring is THE SALES DEPARTMENT 0171 (if outside London) 973 9000.